MISSING ON SUPERSTITION MOUNTAIN

ELISE BROACH

ILLUSTRATED BY
ANTONIO JAVIER CAPARO

Christy Ottaviano Books
Henry Holt and Company
New York

Henry Holt and Company, LLC
Publishers since 1866
175 Fifth Avenue
New York, New York 10010
mackids.com

Library of Congress Cataloging-in-Publication Data
Broach, Elise.
Missing on Superstition Mountain / Elise Broach;
illustrated by Antonio Javier Caparo.—1st ed.
p.   cm.
"Christy Ottaviano Books."
Summary: When brothers Simon, Henry, and Jack move with their parents to Arizona,
they are irresistably drawn to explore the aptly named Superstition Mountain,
in spite of warnings that it is not safe.
ISBN 978-0-8050-9047-5 (hc)
[1. Mountains—Fiction.   2. Brothers—Fiction.   3. Superstition Mountains
(Ariz.)—Fiction.   4. Arizona—Fiction.   5. Mystery and detective stories.]
I. Caparo, Antonio Javier, ill.   II. Title.
PZ7.B78083Mi 2011   [Fic]—dc22   2010049007

First Edition—2011 / Designed by Patrick Collins
Printed in May 2011 in the United States of America by
R. R. Donnelley & Sons Company, Harrisonburg, Virginia.

1 3 5 7 9 10 8 6 4 2

For my nephews,
Nate and Jebbie Bauer

ALSO BY **ELISE BROACH**

Shakespeare's Secret

Desert Crossing

Masterpiece

MISSING ON SUPERSTITION MOUNTAIN

CHAPTER 1

JOSIE RUNS AWAY

THE DAY JOSIE RAN AWAY was the beginning of everything—the bones in the canyon, the haunted mountain, the buried treasure, the town full of secrets—but the Barker boys didn't know it then. All they knew was that Josie was missing, *again,* and they had to find her. It would be harder here, in this strange place in the middle of the desert. But they had no idea how hard, or what else they would find while they were looking.

Josie and the Barker boys had just moved to an old brown-shingled house in Superstition, Arizona, a town in the shadow of an enormous, craggy mountain called Superstition Mountain. So far, the Barker boys didn't much like it. The house itself was all right. It had belonged to their great-uncle, Hank Cormody, or "crazy Uncle Hank" as Mr. Barker called him. Uncle Hank was a former cattle wrangler, gambler, and scout for the U.S. Cavalry, who had shockingly left the house to Mr. Barker in his will when he died at the ripe old age of eighty-six. The timing for a move was good. Mr. Barker's stonemasonry business in Chicago was slowing down—cause for many worrisome, muffled, late-night conversations between Mr. and Mrs. Barker when they thought the boys weren't listening. Since Mrs. Barker was a medical illustrator who could paint pictures of arthritic hips and diseased kidneys anywhere, a hasty decision had been made that a free house in a cheap part of the country was exactly what the Barker family needed.

Which, mostly, it was. The house had a bedroom for each of the boys and a big finished basement, one side of which was crammed full of Uncle Hank's belongings (taped boxes and musty furniture that Mrs. Barker had banished from the upstairs). On the wall was a dartboard, which was a nice surprise because Mrs. Barker never would let the boys get a dartboard, but she could hardly say no when one was hanging right there, with a fistful of pointy darts in the center. Another good thing: Uncle Hank's backyard didn't end in another backyard, or a street, or a driveway, like other backyards. It ended in a vast, rolling nothingness of hills and fields. The boys liked that—the sense that there were no limits, and if somebody hit a ball over the scrubby border of trees and bushes, it might go sailing on forever.

But . . . well, there were lots of buts. The house was far from their friends in Chicago. It was far from the park where they played baseball. It was far from the hill where they used to sled and have snowball fights in the winter. Why, Arizona didn't even have winters! What kind of place didn't have snow? Worst of all, their new house was in this strange town, full of strange people, where nobody looked or talked or seemed the least bit like the people back home.

"It's just because you don't know them yet," their father said. But even their mother, who was annoyingly upbeat about nearly everything, had to admit the town of Superstition lived up to its name. When the middle Barker boy, Henry, said, "The people here are *shifty*," she laughed—because she always laughed at Henry's funny words—but after a minute, she nodded and said, "You know, that is a very good word for it."

There were three Barker boys. Simon, the oldest, was eleven. He had spiky brown hair and a curious, science-y personality, which led to many interesting ideas and experiments. But he could be an annoying know-it-all, and greedy at times. Jack, the youngest, was six. He was hands down the bravest, not just about little things like spiders, but about crashing his bike and jumping from high places. Jack, however, had a temper and would rather take a swing at somebody than work things out peacefully.

In the middle was Henry, age ten, a year younger than Simon and four whole years older than Jack. But because Henry was small and slight and Jack was big and sturdy, people always assumed Henry and Jack were around the same age. This was quite embarrassing to Henry . . . almost as bad as when he was five and his long, curly hair had led everybody to think he was a girl. Henry loved to read and to use the strange words he found in books, though not always the right way. Also, while Henry got along with nearly everybody, he had never had a best friend. (Mrs. Barker said, "Oh, Hen . . . look at your father! He's forty-one and he STILL doesn't have a best friend." Somehow, that wasn't very comforting.)

One last thing about Henry: he was named for Uncle Hank, who was really Henry Cormody, though how the name Henry got turned into Hank was a mystery to the boys (doubtless following the same strange logic by which Sarah became Sally or Margaret became Peggy). Mr. Barker had idolized Uncle Hank when he was young, marking time between his rare visits, eagerly soaking up stories of his adventures, and much later, proudly passing along the name Henry to his middle son. Even at the best of times, Henry felt the weight of this inheritance quite heavily. His great-uncle had been a wild one. He roped cattle, gambled away his money in gloomy saloons, fought bandits with fists and guns, and explored the roughest and most remote stretches of the West on his big spotted Appaloosa horse for the army. Henry, in addition to being small and occasionally mistaken for a girl, was not wild at all. Which made him feel that he should have been named something more regular, like John or David.

The final member of the Barker family was Josie. Was she the boys' sister? No. Their nanny? Definitely not! In fact, Henry often thought that if you were to compare Josie to Nana, the dog nanny in the book *Peter Pan*, you would quickly see that there was *no* comparison. Josie was the Barkers' cat, and she had little interest in taking care of anybody, least of all the three Barker boys. She had been with Mr. and Mrs. Barker for a very long time, and she was vaguely put out that the boys existed at all.

Josie was mostly black, with a patch of white on her neck shaped like Florida. She did not enjoy being squeezed or picked up (though that didn't keep Jack from squeezing and picking her up). Henry liked to say she was *dextrous*, which meant she could open doors and grab things with her paws. Most importantly, she was good at leaping and climbing.

On the day Josie ran away, the boys were sitting on their deck after lunch, staring glumly at the pebbly stretch of backyard, trying to think of something to do. Superstition did not have much to offer. The town center consisted of a library, a grocery store, a gas station, a diner, a town hall with the police and fire stations, a post office, and Coronado Elementary School, which went all the way up to the eighth grade. There were a couple of businesses, too—a car repair place and Mr. Barker's masonry shop. But that was it. Rows of houses sprang up in a square grid around the main avenue through town, and surrounding them? Only barren desert. Even the high school was miles away, in the town of Terra Calde.

This was the first week of summer, and half of the Barkers' neighborhood appeared to have left on vacation.

Not that it mattered, as Henry pointed out; the boys hadn't made any friends since they moved in at the beginning of June, happily missing their last week of school back in Chicago. Here in Arizona, they were on their own.

"We could play cards," Henry suggested.

"Too boring," said Simon.

"We could play Frisbee," said Jack.

"Too windy," said Simon.

"We could go see Dad," said Henry.

Simon shook his head. "Remember what happened last time?"

Mr. Barker's work involved building walls, patios, and walkways. Most of his big jobs were in Phoenix, but he had a few projects in Superstition and the neighboring towns. The boys liked to visit him while he was working, especially whenever he needed help with the cement. But the last time that hadn't turned out so well . . . Jack's sneaker ended up permanently cast in a stretch of sidewalk.

They sat and thought a bit longer.

"I know," Simon declared. "Let's play Mexican prison. Jack, you crawl under the deck. Henry and I will be the guards—" He was just starting to elaborate when Josie, who had been lying peacefully in the warm sun, leapt to her feet and darted across the yard, straight through the clump of scraggly trees, in the direction of Superstition Mountain.

"Where's she going?" Jack demanded. "Josie!" He jumped up and ran after her.

Henry glanced at the house. Technically, they were not supposed to leave their yard. And they were especially not supposed to go up Superstition Mountain. Their parents were very strict about the mountain.

"Jack!" Simon warned. He looked at Henry and shrugged. "Josie doesn't know her way around here. She might get lost." He ran after Jack, calling over his shoulder, "You tell Mom."

Henry scowled. He was often put in the position of breaking bad news to one or the other of his parents, because Simon considered it beneath him to relay information and Jack couldn't be relied upon to get the message right. Henry yanked open the sliding glass door and yelled in the vague direction of his mother's study, "Mom, Josie ran away and we're going after her!" He slammed the door to her faint, "You boys stay close to the house."

Henry crossed the yard, then trotted up the rough slope of the foothills. Giant saguaro cactuses rose from the sandy ground, their prickly arms held upright, like soldiers saluting. The reddish brown peaks and bluffs of Superstition Mountain loomed in the distance. Henry could see Simon and Jack—and Josie far ahead, a black streak against the light earth. Where *was* she going? That was the thing about Josie. You never knew what she was thinking. Sometimes when Henry stroked her head, she'd purr with lazy pleasure and then, a minute later, hiss and bat his hand with her claws.

He caught up with his brothers, who'd stopped running. June in Arizona was fiercely hot, not like Illinois. At least there was a wind today . . . even if it blew dry dust in their faces. Simon and Jack were yelling for Josie, but Henry couldn't see her anywhere. She never came when they called anyway.

"Where'd she go?" Henry asked, squinting into the hills, past the spiked grasses and bright yellow clumps of wildflowers. The strong sun made crisp shadows on the ground.

"She climbed over those rocks." Simon ran his hand through his hair till it stood up even more. The boys gathered in an uncertain huddle, staring at Superstition Mountain.

They all knew Superstition Mountain was off-limits.

But it wasn't clear why. Their mom had said something about mountain lions and rattlesnakes. Their dad just said they could get lost.

Jack scrambled on top of a boulder. "I see her!" he said. "She's way up there. Come on!"

CHAPTER 2

UP THE MOUNTAIN

HENRY HESITATED. "Do you think it's okay to go up the mountain?"

Simon considered for a moment. "Look, there's kind of a trail. We can break off branches from the bushes and stick them in the ground so we can find our way back."

That sounded like something Uncle Hank might have done in his army scout days, Henry thought. Reassured, he began breaking branches off the brittle shrubs and propping them in the ground as they walked, avoiding the sharp spines of the prickly pears and giant cactuses.

"They look like big, skinny people," Henry told Jack.

"Yeah, needle people," Jack said.

"Think if your skin was covered in prickers like that," Simon said. "Like a porcupine. You could scare people away just by brushing against them."

"Cool!" Jack said, and proceeded to pretend he was covered in prickers, bumping into Simon and Henry until Simon threatened to push him into a cactus.

When Henry turned back, their house had sunk from view. But the zigzag line of sticks poked up from the dirt, as certain as mile markers on a highway.

Soon the slope became steeper and rockier. Jack still ran ahead, but Henry could hear him panting from the effort. Lizards skittered across the sandy ground. Henry grabbed the sharp edges of boulders to pull himself up, the sun hot on his back, sweat coursing down his forehead. The trail turned back on itself. It faded into thickets of brush, then reappeared. They kept climbing.

"Look at that funny rock," Jack said after a while, pointing to a narrow spire that stood alone in the maze of bluffs.

Simon nodded in recognition. "That's Weaver's Needle. Dad showed it to me. It's a landmark."

"What's a landmark?" Jack wanted to know.

"A part of the land that stands out," Henry explained. "You can use it to tell where you are." That's what scouts did, didn't they? They remembered landmarks so they could guide people in the wilderness. He tried to memorize the position of Weaver's Needle.

"So where are we?" Jack wanted to know.

Henry looked around at the twisty, boulder-strewn landscape. "I don't know."

They climbed on. Behind them the flat land stretched, speckled with the distant houses of Superstition and divided by a thin stripe of highway. Ahead lay the tangle of cliffs and peaks.

After a while, Jack asked fretfully, "Do you see Josie?"

Henry shook his head. Had she really come all the way up here? It seemed like they'd left home a long time ago.

Overhead, a large dark bird wheeled against the blue sky.

"Is that a hawk?" Henry asked Simon.

"Yeah," Simon said. "Or a vulture."

Henry shuddered.

Simon kicked at the dry ground, scattering pebbles. A fat gray toad jumped out from under a rock.

"Look!" Jack cried, pointing. None of them were used to the strange desert creatures, so different from the squirrels and robins of Chicago. It reminded Henry of *The Swiss Family Robinson*, a book he'd read about people marooned on a Pacific island who were always bumping into exotic wildlife.

Simon, who would usually have been intrigued by the toad, barely glanced at it. "We should have brought water," he said, staring at the cloud of dust where his sneaker had been.

They kept climbing. There were a few trees now, and the sunlight filtered through, dappling the ground. The boys stopped to catch their breath. The mountain's loneliness filled the air with small, mysterious sounds . . . the high twittering of birds, the rustling of branches.

Jack poked through the brush, and Simon snapped, "Don't go off the trail, Jack."

"But I can't see Josie anymore."

Henry collapsed against a boulder. The sun had shifted in the sky. "I don't like it up here," he said. "It's . . . it's *eerie*."

Simon turned to him. "What are you scared of? Mountain lions?"

"No," Henry protested. He *was* a little scared of mountain lions, not to mention rattlesnakes, but it was more than that. The quiet was creepy. It felt like they were being watched. Like the mountain was holding its breath.

Simon climbed up on Henry's rock for a better view, shading his eyes with his hand. He looked like a real explorer, Henry thought enviously. "There's no sign of Josie," he said after a minute. "We should go back."

"And leave her here by herself?" Henry was horrified. He wanted to go home, but how could they abandon Josie?

"Yeah!" Jack ran down the path to where they were sitting. "We can't do that! Mom says there are mountain lions! What if she gets EATEN?"

"Eaten?" Simon snorted. "What's going to eat Josie? She can take care of herself."

"Back home she could," Henry said. "But here is different. She's not used to it." Henry thought about how he'd feel if his brothers left him alone on the mountain when it was getting dark. Despite the heat, he shivered.

Simon looked exasperated. "Hen, we don't have any water. That's what people die of in places like this, not mountain lions."

Jack started to climb the boulder. "Make room for me." He pushed Simon's leg.

Simon frowned at him. "No. It's too crowded."

"Is not."

"Is too."

"Is NOT." Jack's foot dug into Henry's back as he crawled past him.

"Hey!" Henry complained.

"Jack, stop—" Simon said, trying to keep his balance.

"Move over," Jack insisted.

"Watch out," Henry cried, as Jack slammed into his shoulder.

But it was too late. Simon took a step to the side just as Jack tried to give him another push, and Jack went tumbling over the top of the boulder.

Crunch! He disappeared in a dense thicket. Then there was a fast crackling sound, and to their horror, Henry and Simon realized Jack hadn't just fallen to the ground—he was rolling down a hill.

"Heeeyyyy!!!" Jack cried.

They could hear his body bumping and thumping against the hard earth.

CHAPTER 3
THE HIDDEN CANYON

HENRY AND SIMON quickly climbed over the boulder and slid down the other side, grabbing at branches so they wouldn't fall. The ground pitched sharply into a narrow canyon, well hidden from view by the rocks and brush.

"Jack?" Henry called.

They stared into the ravine. Its rock walls were steep and reddish brown in the fading sun, with stunted shrubs growing here and there. The ground was sixty or seventy feet below, a thin strip of pebbles broken by gray-green bushes and small trees. It looked as if there'd been a stream down there once, but now it was only a dry, stony path. The wind whistled forlornly through the narrow chute.

"Jack!" Simon bellowed, his voice echoing off the canyon walls.

Finally, Jack's voice drifted up to them. "I'm down here!"

Henry could see sunlight flashing off Jack's sandy brown hair several yards below. He was huddled on a ledge.

"Don't move!" Henry yelled. "You look like you're . . . *precarious*."

"No, I'm not!" Jack yelled back. "But I might fall."

"That's what it means," Henry answered.

"Oh," Jack said. "Say it normal. And I'd better not fall, or I'll be all broken up in pieces. It's a long way to the bottom."

"Hold on, we're coming." Simon began scooting down the canyon wall. "Are you okay?"

Henry gingerly followed, gripping one tree branch, then another, to keep from slipping.

"I think so," Jack mumbled. "But hurry up!"

A minute later, they were together on the ledge—a slab of rock, jutting into the air high above the canyon floor. When he peered over the side, Henry felt sick to his stomach.

Jack, meanwhile, was covered in dirt, with bits of twigs and grass strewn through his hair. "Owwww!" he moaned. "That hurt."

"Yeah, well, serves you right for trying to knock me off," Simon complained.

"Simon," Henry warned, seeing the look on Jack's face. That was the thing about Jack; he could go from fine to furious in less time than it took to call him a baby. He was kind of like Josie that way.

"We should head back," Henry said quickly. "It'll be dark soon." He glanced at the sky. If the sun went down, they wouldn't even be able to see the sticks that were meant to guide them home.

Then something caught his eye. A few feet away, on the edge of rock hanging over the canyon, there were three round, white objects, like very big softballs, plunked in a row.

"What are those?" he asked, leaning forward on his knees.

Simon stood up slowly, pressing one hand against the rock wall. "Yeah, what *are* those?"

Jack crawled over and picked one up.

"It looks like a—" he began, turning it over.

They all gasped.

It was a skull.

A human skull.

CHAPTER 4
WHICH WAY?

THE SKULL WAS BLEACHED from the sun, with yawning eye sockets and a single crowded row of teeth. Henry froze. Jack was so startled he almost dropped it. Wide-eyed, he set it gently on the ground, where it grinned fiercely back at them.

Henry had seen the skulls their mother drew for medical textbooks and journals—pale shadowy orbs with vacant eye holes and grim, toothy smiles. But somehow seeing one for real was different.

"What's that doing here?" Henry's voice quaked.

"I don't know," Simon said. "But look . . . there are three of them." He walked carefully to the edge of the rocky outcropping and lifted another of the skulls, turning it over in his hands. "Mom would love this," he said softly.

Henry could tell Simon was trying to act like he wasn't scared, which somehow made him feel worse. Gently, he picked up the third skull. It was heavier than he expected, with thick wavy lines crossing the top.

"It looks like it was glued together," he whispered.

"They're all that way," Simon said, tracing a finger over one of the seams. "Those lines are where the skull comes together after your brain grows to full size."

How did Simon know this stuff? Simon saw Henry's look and shrugged. "Mom told me."

"What's this, then?" Henry asked, rubbing his finger over a shallow depression in the bone. It looked like a dent in a Ping-Pong ball.

"Huh." Simon set down the skull he was holding and took Henry's. "That's interesting. The others don't have that."

"It's bashed in," Jack announced. "Like this—wham!" He walloped Henry's arm.

"Ow!" Henry gasped. "Cut it out, Jack." He touched the curve of the indentation. "It's so smooth," he said.

"I think we should put them back," Simon said suddenly. He squatted at the edge of the rocky ledge, arranging the three skulls exactly where the boys had found them. Then he stood, brushed his hands on his pants,

and squinted at the wall of the canyon. "Let's go. It'll be dark soon."

Henry stood where he was, mesmerized by the skulls. "It's like they're looking at something in the canyon," he whispered. "All lined up like that." The skulls were poised on the lip of rock, facing out over the void.

"Do you think . . ." Jack swallowed. "Do you think a mountain lion killed them?"

"And what? Put their heads in a row like this? Come on, Jack," Simon scoffed.

Jack glowered at him. "Well, how'd they die? Something killed them."

Henry felt a chill of foreboding. "And there are three of them," he said slowly. "Like the three of us."

"Henry." Simon shot him a warning glance. "You're freaking out Jack."

But Henry couldn't help it. Here they were, in this lonely, secret place, with the heads of three dead people. He thought of how he'd yelled good-bye to his mom hours earlier, when they ran after Josie. She was illustrating a book on sports injuries, and he could picture her bent over her drafting table, gently sketching the contours of a shoulder or elbow. He wished he'd gone inside and hugged her.

"What if they got stuck and DIED here?" Jack said. "What if we can't get out?"

"That's dumb," Simon said impatiently. "We got *into* the canyon, didn't we?"

Jack frowned at him, but Henry could see his mouth quivering, as if he might cry.

Simon saw it too; he relented. "Look, Jack." He brushed dust off the ridges of one skull. "It's pretty clean. And white, from the sun. So you can tell it's been here a long time. This is somebody who died years ago."

"Three people," Henry whispered.

"Yeah," Simon said.

"Should we—" Henry stopped. "Do you think we should take them back with us?"

"And do what? Show Mom and Dad?" Simon wiped his hands on his pants. "We aren't even allowed to be up here."

"Yeah." Jack's eyes widened. "We'll get in trouble. And they won't let us near this place ever again."

Henry wasn't so sure he wanted to go near this place ever again. But Josie was here—somewhere—and what if she couldn't find her way home? They would have to come back to look for her. Henry bit his lip. "But we shouldn't just leave them, should we?"

Simon thought for a minute. "I bet they've been here for years and years, Hen. A while longer won't make any difference." He wedged his foot into the rock and started to haul himself back up the slope. "C'mon, let's go."

Jack waffled. "What about Josie?"

Henry pulled Jack to his feet. "We won't be able to find her in the dark anyway. And Mom will worry if we aren't back by dinner." He watched Simon's red shirt moving up the side of the ravine. "Josie will be okay for one night," he decided. "She was gone overnight lots of times at the old house, remember?"

"Yeah," Jack said doubtfully, "but there were no mountain lions in Illinois."

Henry boosted Jack onto the rocky slope above the ledge. They followed Simon, crawling on their knees, grabbing at rocks and shrubs. Henry glanced back, once, at the three white skulls staring out over the gorge. Who did they belong to? How had they gotten there?

The wind made its mournful sound, sweeping through the canyon as the boys clambered back onto the trail.

"Hurry," Simon said. "It's almost dark."

Henry ran after Simon, urging Jack to keep up.

"Do you think there are more mountain lions in the day or at night?" Jack asked.

"It's the same, probably," Simon said. "But I think you have to worry about rattlesnakes more during the day, when it's warm."

At least that was something, thought Henry.

The trail forked up ahead. Simon paused. "It's this way, right?" he asked Henry.

"Where are the sticks?" Henry peered down each twisting, narrow path. It was hard to even call them paths.

"This way," Simon decided, scanning the darkening sky.

They started running again, stumbling over the rough ground, the big brown rocks crowding around them. Henry could feel his heart thumping in his chest. Shouldn't they be near the bottom by now? The mountain seemed to have no end. And the feeling was there, still—not just of being watched . . . almost of being chased.

They ran faster. Jack fell twice, but he scrambled back to his feet without stopping.

"I don't think this is right," Henry said to Simon. "I don't remember it."

"We're going downhill, so it must be right," Simon answered. But he stopped, scanning the trail behind them, and the boys huddled together, breathing loudly.

"There shouldn't be trees here," Henry said. "Most of the way up, it was all rocks and bushes, remember?"

The sun was almost gone now. The color of the sky had changed to lavender. Henry heard a strange creaking sound.

"What's that?" he whispered.

But before anyone could answer, the creaking grew louder and there was a sharp crack, like a gunshot. Henry jumped and Simon yelled, "Look out!"

CHAPTER 5

"STAY OFF THE MOUNTAIN!"

HENRY FELT HIMSELF HIT the ground, with Simon on top of him, and he couldn't understand what was happening. When he opened his eyes, he was lying in the dirt on the trail. Simon leaned over him.

"Henry?"

Henry sat up slowly. Ahead of them, blocking the trail, was a large tree branch. It had crashed down only a few feet away.

"It must have been the wind," Simon said, squinting up at the tree.

"It almost smushed you!" Jack cried.

"Come on." Simon pulled Henry to his feet. "Climb over it. We've got to keep going." Henry shuddered, crawling over the branch after his brothers, his knees scraping the rough bark.

They began to run again.

Henry could almost feel the mountain grabbing at them and sense its disappointment that they were getting away.

Finally, they saw a stick, upright in the dirt. They'd gotten off their trail somehow, but here they were back on it. Simon's face relaxed. "We're almost there! Look!"

And sure enough, past the barren foothills, Henry could see the twinkling lights of the houses in their neighborhood. He glanced nervously back at the mountain.

"Poor Josie," he said quietly.

"Yeah," Simon said. "But she'll be okay. She always is."

The boys ran the rest of the way, over the empty fields, past the tall cactuses standing watch at the edge of their yard. As they tromped onto the deck, Henry skidded to a halt. In the bright kitchen, he could see Mr. and Mrs. Barker, sober-faced, talking to a policeman. They hadn't even reached the door when Mr. Barker yanked it open, his face awash in relief. "Where *were* you boys?" he demanded, pulling them inside.

Simon shot Henry a warning glance, which Henry instantly understood. They couldn't say anything about where they'd been. Their parents were clearly freaked out already. But what was going on? They'd been late for dinner lots of times in Illinois, and nobody had ever called the police.

Mrs. Barker clasped Jack against her waist. "Oh, I was so worried! Henry, I told you not to go far. What happened?"

The policeman, a heavy man in a navy-blue uniform, leaned on the kitchen counter waiting for their answer. He didn't look unfriendly, exactly, Henry decided. But his hands were as big as baseball mitts.

"We . . ." Henry took a deep breath. "We were just trying to catch Josie. She ran out of the yard, and we followed her. But . . . but we couldn't find her."

Mr. Barker folded his arms, looking from Henry to Simon. "Did you boys go up the mountain?" he asked evenly, sounding merely curious. That was a trap, Henry knew. If they said yes, the whole kitchen would explode.

Jack said, "Well, Josie—"

Henry shook his head quickly. Jack was easily fooled. Simon interjected, "Josie ran through the bushes out back, so we followed her. Not up the mountain, just into those little hills. We got lost and couldn't find our way back."

Henry nodded vigorously. "As soon as we saw the lights, we came straight home. *Directly.*"

Now it was Mr. and Mrs. Barker's turn to exchange glances. "You didn't go up that mountain?" Mr. Barker asked again, looking at Jack.

"Nope," Jack insisted. "But we think Josie did! And there are mountain lions, aren't there, Mom? Isn't that what you said? And rattlesnakes too!" His eyes widened. "Do you think she'll be okay?"

Mrs. Barker ran her fingers through Jack's hair, picking out bits of leaves and dirt. "What's all this?" she asked, crouching down to look at him. "Jack, did you fall?" Behind her glasses, her worried brown eyes made Henry cringe.

But Jack brushed her off. "I just tripped," he said stoutly. "What about Josie?"

"Listen to me, boys." The policeman straightened and crossed the kitchen floor in two strides. Henry saw that he had a bright silver badge and a leather holster that bulged with a gun, just like a real policeman.

"You scared your mom and dad, you know that?" He loomed over them.

Simon and Henry nodded. Jack asked, "Is that a real gun?"

"It certainly is," the policeman said. "And I'll tell you what else: I've had to use it. Up on Superstition Mountain."

The boys looked at each other. "You have?" Henry asked faintly.

"Yes, I have." He paused, and exchanged a long look with Henry's parents. It occurred to Henry that a whole separate conversation was going on between the grown-ups—one without any words. The policeman bent down now, hands on his knees, his broad, stern face inches from Henry's. "You don't want to be going up there. It's not safe. Understand?"

Henry gulped. He tried not to stare at the dark pores that speckled the man's nose.

"What did you shoot at?" Jack asked. "A mountain lion?"

"That's not important," the policeman said. "What's important is that you boys STAY OFF THE MOUNTAIN!"

He said this last part so forcefully that Henry backed up against his mother. Even Simon looked shaken.

"We will, okay?" Simon said. "We just went looking for Josie. We didn't go up any mountain." He turned on Mr. Barker accusingly. "Don't you trust us?"

Henry was a little awed by this show of boldness, which made their parents' suspicions seem petty and unfair.

Mr. Barker frowned. "Yes, of course we do. But I know how you guys feel about that cat."

"How we all feel about that cat," Mrs. Barker corrected him, continuing to run her fingers through Jack's hair, dislodging the remnants of the gulch. "I'm sure Josie will find her way back," she said soothingly. "She's got more brains than half the people I know. She'll get hungry and be home before bedtime."

Henry sighed. He fervently hoped his mother was right. But she hadn't been up the mountain. She didn't know the way the place could hold on to you.

"Thanks for coming out, Officer Myers," Mr. Barker said, ushering the policeman into the entryway, with Jack trotting along, clamoring to see the squad car. Henry followed.

"Oh, it's no trouble," the policeman said, his gaze darting past Henry into the living room and hallway. "I was curious to see what you'd done to old Hank's place. I haven't been out here in years. Left you some of his things, did he?"

"Too many of his things, if you ask my wife," Mr.

Barker said ruefully. "Most of them are in the basement. Did you know my uncle?"

Henry leaned in eagerly.

"Not personally," Officer Myers amended. "But everybody knew him. He was quite a character. Lots of stories about ol' Hank Cormody."

"Like what?" Henry asked.

The policeman laughed. "Well, I'm not sure many of them can be repeated in this company."

Henry suspected that meant something about women, because Uncle Hank was known to have had a number of girlfriends, more than one at the same time. ("Your Uncle Hank was a player," Mrs. Barker told Henry once, in a disapproving voice, and it was clear she didn't mean playing sports or board games or music, things you would ordinarily be proud of.)

"Aren't there any stories you could tell us?" Henry asked, hoping for a quiet kind of story that would make him feel like he and Uncle Hank had something in common.

Officer Myers thought for a minute. "Well, there was that time he pinned a rattlesnake with a screwdriver."

Henry's eyes widened.

"Really?" Simon interrupted. "How'd he do that?"

The policeman scratched his head. "As I heard it, he'd been working on the house"—he gestured past the front door—"fixing the siding or something out front, and he must have disturbed a rattler in the bushes. When it pulled back to strike, he hurled his screwdriver right at it and pinned its neck to the ground—bam!" The policeman smacked the side of his hand against his open palm.

"Cool!" Simon said, and Jack blurted out, "Wow!"

Henry said nothing, thinking that he was not sure he would even recognize a rattlesnake, and he certainly would not be able to pin it to the ground with a screwdriver.

"Well, from what they say, ol' Hank was a fair hand at darts."

The boys glanced at one another.

"Ha! That he was," Mr. Barker said fondly.

"All right, boys," Mrs. Barker called from the kitchen. "Time for dinner and bed."

"I'm sorry we bothered you for nothing." Mr. Barker swung open the front door. The boys gathered around him.

"Not at all. It was nice to meet you folks," Officer Myers replied. "And welcome to Superstition. How do you like it so far?"

"Well, it's only been a couple of weeks." Mr. Barker gestured to the wall of cardboard moving boxes, still stacked in the living room. "But we like it a lot. It's got a great sense of history."

Officer Myers stopped, his hand on the front door. "What kind of history?"

"The surrounding area," Mr. Barker explained. "It feels like the Old West. I understand there's a ghost town not far from here."

A ghost town! Henry perked up. Simon raised his eyebrows. "With real ghosts?" Jack asked.

Mr. Barker laughed. "No, Jack. It's an old frontier town that's been abandoned."

The policeman paused. "Well, that's another place that should be strictly off-limits for your boys. Those buildings are in terrible shape. They could collapse at any minute."

"Of course," Mr. Barker agreed. "I'll make sure they don't go anywhere near there."

Officer Myers stepped onto the front porch, then turned to Mr. Barker, his broad face shining in the porch light. "The mountain," he said quietly. "It's tempting to the kids around here . . . they all want to be little explorers." He stopped, glancing down at Jack. "But it isn't safe. Remember that."

Henry thought he seemed about to say more. Was he still talking about the mountain lions and rattlesnakes? Or something else?

"Right," Mr. Barker said. "Thanks again."

A moment later, Henry heard an engine roar and saw the police car back down the driveway, its blue lights pulsing in the chilly, black night.

"Boys! It's late. I mean it," their mother scolded, herding them out of the entryway.

Jack craned to see the lights. "Wow . . . cool!"

Henry would have thought it was cool too, if he weren't so worried about Josie. She was out there somewhere, alone in the desert night. Alone on the mountain with the three skulls—the mountain that had almost captured them, too.

CHAPTER 6
A NEW PLAN

JOSIE DIDN'T COME BACK at bedtime. She didn't come back the next morning, or the next afternoon, or anytime the next day. The boys put a bowl of her tuna-flavored kibbles on the back deck, in case she showed up when nobody was home. But each time they checked, the bowl was untouched.

On Thursday, three days after Josie had disappeared, Simon, Henry, and Jack sat on the back deck staring morosely at the empty yard. Henry had been trying to read—he was halfway through *Treasure Island* and imagining himself kidnapped on a pirate ship—but it was hard to concentrate with Josie missing and in danger.

"What if a mountain lion ate her?" Jack asked sadly.

"I don't think they eat other cats," Simon said. "That would be too weird."

"Yeah," said Henry. "Like *cannibalism*."

But he wasn't so sure. For a mountain lion, was eating a cat any different than eating a raccoon or a squirrel? They were all just tasty pieces of meat, weren't they?

"Do you think we should go back up there and look for her?" Henry said this softly, afraid that Mrs. Barker, who was unloading the dishwasher, would hear.

Simon scanned the jagged silhouette of Superstition Mountain. "Maybe," he said. "But we can't go anytime soon. Mom and Dad are still too nervous."

It was true that their parents had been unusually watchful and attentive for the last few days. Mrs. Barker stopped work to check on them frequently, even when they were only playing in the driveway, and when Mr. Barker came home at night, he required a full account of their day.

"They're like prison guards," Simon complained. "We can't do anything."

There were two things the boys wanted to do: find Josie and figure out the real danger of Superstition Mountain. Henry and Simon had quickly decided that however scary mountain lions and rattlesnakes might be, their parents and the policeman were worried about something else entirely. What was it?

"There's something they're not telling us," Simon said.

"Yeah," Henry agreed. "They're being sneaky, like those people in movies who pretend they don't know anything about the crime. You know, when the police *interrogate* them."

Of course, there was also something Henry, Simon, and Jack weren't telling Mr. and Mrs. Barker. They'd said nothing about the three skulls. At night, before Henry fell asleep, he could see them clearly: ghostly white blobs perched on the ledge overlooking the canyon. He was sure those skulls had a story to tell . . . especially the one with the dent in it.

Mrs. Barker opened the sliding door and looked down at them, hands on her hips. "Boys, come on. I know you're upset about Josie, but I still think she's okay. Don't you remember in Illinois, that time she was gone for a week? She came back all fat and happy, like she'd been on vacation."

Henry smiled a little. It was true. They'd been so worried about her, but when she finally appeared at the back door, she was round and well-rested. She didn't even seem particularly glad to be home.

Mrs. Barker picked up Henry's neglected book and tucked the bookmark securely in place. "It's only been three days, Hen. She'll come back."

"Hey!" Simon jumped to his feet. "I know! We can make flyers with her picture on them and put them up around the neighborhood."

"That's a good idea," Mrs. Barker coaxed them. "I'll get you some markers. Why don't you work at the kitchen table?"

She returned with a fistful of colored markers and some blank paper. "Now I have to get to work too, okay? So no interruptions, please. I'm on deadline for that book on sports medicine, and I have several drawings I have to finish by the end of the week."

When she left the room, Simon whispered, "Finally she'll be out of our hair." Henry hoped so. They all much preferred their mother busy with work than nosing around in their affairs.

Glad to have something to do, they huddled over the blank paper.

"I'll draw a picture of her!" Jack announced cheerfully, grabbing a thick black marker.

"Jack—" Simon started to protest.

"Let me do it," Jack insisted. "I'm a good drawer."

He knelt on a chair and leaned over the table, pressing hard with the marker. Henry saw his face scrunch with concentration; his tongue kept slipping out of the side of his mouth while he worked. When he finished, he waved the picture jubilantly under Simon's nose. "See!"

Simon snorted. "That doesn't look at all like Josie. That looks like a big black cow."

Jack balled up his fist, and Henry barely had time to duck as he reached out to whack Simon's arm. "Does not!"

"Moooo," Simon said.

"Boys," Mrs. Barker called from her study.

"Mom!" Jack yelled. "Simon's being mean!"

"Simon—" Mrs. Barker began.

"I am not! Jack hit me."

"Jack—" Mrs. Barker said sternly.

"I drew Josie and he said it looks like a cow!"

"It doesn't look like a cow," Henry ventured. "It looks like a goat."

"All right, all right." Mrs. Barker appeared in the doorway. "Stop fighting! What did I just say about not interrupting me?"

Simon whipped the paper out of Jack's hand. "Look, Mom. Does this look anything like Josie? If we put this up around the neighborhood, everyone will think we lost a black cow." He studied Jack's drawing. "With horns. A bull."

"Hey!" Jack cried. "Give that back!"

"That is ENOUGH." Mrs. Barker took the drawing and put it on the counter. "Why don't you use a photo of Josie instead? We can copy it right onto the paper. Take one off the fridge. When you're finished, I'll make photocopies for you in the study. But no more fighting! Understand?"

"Yeah, Mom, sorry," Simon said, but Henry could see him press his foot down on Jack's beneath the table.

Henry took a photo of Josie off the fridge—it was one of her lying on the couch at their old house, with a smug expression on her face—and carefully taped it to a blank piece of paper. Below the photo, Simon wrote in neat capital letters

MISSING
BLACK CAT*
VERY FRIENDLY

At the bottom, he added in small print *WHITE SPOT ON NECK.

"Okay, how does that look?" Simon held the paper aloft for their review.

"That's really good!" Jack said happily, the cow episode already forgotten. "Now let's make lots and lots of copies and put them up *everywhere*."

Henry scrutinized the flyer. "I don't think Josie's VERY friendly. Just friendly."

Simon considered. "Okay." He carefully crossed out *very*.

"And what's the reward?"

Simon shrugged. "I don't know. But we need a reward. Nobody will pay any attention to our signs otherwise."

"Do we have to use our own money?" Henry asked anxiously. He had twenty-four dollars in his piggybank, but he was saving up for the complete trilogy of *The Lord of the Rings*.

"Course not," Simon scoffed. "Mom will pay it."

They carried the poster to her study, where Mrs. Barker was leaning over her drawing table, pencil poised. She looked up. "All set?"

Simon showed her the paper. "You'll give a reward if somebody brings back Josie, right?"

"Well, yes, I guess that would be okay," she said. "You didn't say an amount, did you?"

"No," Simon said. "It's better not to, because then people might think we're really rich and the reward is a lot of money."

Mrs. Barker smiled. "This looks terrific! You did a nice job, all of you. I'll copy it right now, and you can ride your bikes around the neighborhood and put it up on telephone poles."

Mrs. Barker placed a sheaf of yellow paper in the tray of the copying machine, which produced a stack of flyers in a matter of minutes. "See? Don't they look nice?"

They looked bright and official, Henry thought . . . but the photo of Josie made him sad. What if they never did find her? He pictured the way she would lie on the couch, with her hind legs scissored across each other, the tip of her tail twitching.

Mrs. Barker gave the stack a brisk pat. "Take the

stapler and some tape, and stay in our neighborhood, okay? Don't cross Coronado Road."

So they set out on their bikes, with three handfuls of flyers and the ardent hope that someone in the neighborhood would recognize Josie's picture and know exactly where she was.

CHAPTER 7
A GLIMPSE OF SOMETHING

AFTER ALMOST TWO HOURS of putting flyers on telephone poles in the broiling heat, all three boys were
exhausted. They'd ridden down every street in the neighborhood. The sun was high in the cloudless sky, hot
on their backs, flashing off cars, leaving them sweaty and
thirsty.

They'd just turned off Coronado Road to head home
when Henry saw something out of the corner of his eye
that made him slam on his brakes. It was a cat, crossing
a front yard. A black cat.

He jumped off the side of his bike, letting it clatter
against the curb.

"Hey! Josie?" he cried. Before he could be sure, a
girl—who looked about his age and had been sitting on

the front porch of the house—leapt to her feet, grabbed the cat, and ran inside.

Simon and Jack circled back to where Henry's bike lay in the gutter. "What happened?" Simon asked. "Did you fall off?"

"No—I think I just saw Josie!"

"You did?" Jack jumped off his bike. "Where?"

Henry stared at the house in bafflement. "Maybe it wasn't, but it sure looked like Josie. A girl just took her inside that house." He pointed at the two-story gray house directly in front of them. It had narrow flower beds on either side of the front stoop, overflowing with spiky plants and pink and orange flowers. A green hose coiled nearby.

Simon lifted his bike onto the sidewalk and pushed down the kickstand. "Let's go see."

They climbed the steps to the porch. "Knock on the door," Simon told Jack.

Jack frowned. "You do it."

"I'll do it," said Henry, but not before Jack stomped on Simon's foot and knocked on the door himself—a *bang, bang, bang* that echoed inside the house. The boys waited.

Jack rang the bell. *Ding-dong. Ding-dong.* The boys waited some more.

"I know she's in there," Henry said. He pressed his

face against the window next to the door. "Hey, I can see the living room." He saw a flowery sofa, a glossy coffee table stacked with magazines, end tables cluttered with framed pictures, and a big, fancy-looking green armchair with gold braiding. "It's very . . . *opulent*."

Simon and Jack crowded behind him. "Does that mean there's a cat in there?" Jack wanted to know.

"Nope," Henry said, disappointed.

"Let me see!" Jack pushed in front of him. "Hey, there *is* a black cat. It's walking down the hall," he said. Then he cried excitedly, "Look! It's Josie!"

"Really?" Simon elbowed between the two of them.

Breathlessly, they watched a black cat wander into the living room and sit down, calmly licking her paws. There was a white patch on her neck shaped like Florida.

"It is Josie!" Simon said. "What's she doing in there?"

Josie was safe! She hadn't been eaten by mountain lions! She hadn't been bitten by a rattlesnake! She'd come down from the mountain all by herself, and she really didn't look any different at all. But what was she doing in this strange house?

Henry pointed. "Look, there's the girl. She's hiding behind that chair."

Behind one side of the green satiny armchair, they

could see pink sneakers, a striped sleeve, and a long, brown braid.

Jack pounded on the door again. "We see you!" he yelled. "Give us back our cat!"

The sneakers didn't move, but the braid swung sideways and half a face appeared. It was a mad face.

"Open the door!" Henry shouted.

"Go away!" yelled the girl. She hid behind the chair again.

Jack tried the handle of the front door but it wouldn't open. "We have to save Josie," he said. "Josie! Josie, come here!"

Josie looked up, gazing at them with her golden eyes. Henry thought she seemed unimpressed.

"Josie!" he yelled.

She started licking her paws again.

The braid moved and the whole face appeared this time. Henry could see a scattering of freckles. "Go away," the girl said loudly, glowering at them. "If you don't, I'll call the police."

Simon was mad now too. "No, we'll call the police! You stole our cat."

"You'll go to JAIL," Jack cried. He made a horrible face and pressed it against the window.

The girl came out from behind the chair and sat down next to Josie, stroking her back. "Leave us alone! You're the ones trespassing. *You'll* go to jail." She stuck out her tongue at Jack.

The three boys looked at one another.

"Who is she?" Henry asked. Since they had moved into Uncle Hank's house right as school was ending, they hadn't met many of the kids in the neighborhood. And now it seemed like everyone was on vacation or away at summer camp. Except this girl, apparently. This horrible, cat-stealing girl.

"I recognize her," Simon said. "She rode her bike in that Pioneer Days parade a couple of weeks ago, remember? It was covered with all those dumb ribbons."

"They weren't dumb!" came from inside the house.

"She can hear you," Henry whispered. "We have to do something. Let's go tell Mom."

"No!" Jack said. "We can't leave Josie. We have to rescue her."

Simon scanned the side of the house. "Let's see if there's another way in," he whispered.

"You go away," the girl said again. She put her arm around Josie, still petting her. Even through the window, the boys could tell that Josie was arching her back and purring.

"Okay, we're leaving," Henry said loudly. The three boys stomped down the porch steps and walked toward the driveway.

"Is she watching us?" Simon asked.

Henry glanced back and shook his head.

"Quick!"

They raced around the side of the house to the back-yard, then up the deck stairs to the sliding glass door. Simon grabbed the handle and pulled, but the door wouldn't budge.

The girl walked into the kitchen, holding Josie in her arms. "Ha!" she said. "It's locked."

Jack pounded on the glass.

"Cut it out," the girl said. "My mom is *napping*. You'll wake her up."

Something about the way she said this made Henry think it wasn't true. He suddenly felt certain she was in the house alone.

"Listen," Simon told her, jabbing his finger against the glass. "That's our cat. She's been missing for three whole days! You can't take somebody else's cat."

The girl held Josie tighter and glared. "It's not your cat. She's a stray. I found her."

"She is not!" Henry cried. "Look at her collar."

The girl didn't move.

"Can't we come in?" Henry asked. "Then we can show you."

Josie continued to gaze at them impassively . . . almost as if they were strangers, Henry had to admit. But then she never was the kind of cat who acted excited to see anybody.

"She's not your cat," the girl repeated stubbornly. She lowered Josie to the kitchen floor, and Josie darted back to the living room.

"Let's go," Simon said to Henry and Jack. "She's not going to give us Josie, and I don't think there's anyone else home." He called over his shoulder. "You'll be sorry. Our mom is going to call your mom, and then you'll be in big trouble."

As they walked across the yard, they heard the door slide open.

"Wait," the girl said.

The boys turned around. "Are you going to give Josie back?" Henry asked.

The girl frowned at him. "Her name is Princess," she said.

Princess! The boys looked at one another in disgust.

Jack balled his fists and started back toward the deck, but Simon grabbed his shoulder.

"Forget it," he said. "Mom will know what to do."

CHAPTER 8

DELILAH

SIMON, HENRY, AND JACK rode their bikes as fast as they could all the way home. They burst through the kitchen door.

"Mom!" Simon shouted.

"Mom, where are you?" Henry called.

"Mom, we need you!" Jack yelled.

They heard their mother's exasperated sigh from the study. After a minute she emerged, pushing her glasses to the bridge of her nose. "All right, all right, here I am," she said. "What's the matter?"

They all began talking at once.

"Mom, somebody took Josie!"

"This girl down the street has her—"

"Josie is TRAPPED—"

"You have to do something!"

Mrs. Barker held up a hand. "Boys, you have to calm down. I can't understand a thing you're saying. One at a time, please."

"Mom!" Henry cried. "A girl has Josie and she's holding her *hostage*."

Just then the doorbell rang. Their mother brushed past them. "Wait a sec. Someone's at the door."

The boys charged after her. When she swung open the front door, there on the stoop was the girl, carrying Josie.

She smiled at Mrs. Barker. "I think I found your cat," she said politely.

"Josie! Are we ever glad to see you!" Mrs. Barker swept Josie into her arms and cuddled her, smiling warmly. "And weren't you sweet to bring her back."

"Hey!" Jack protested. "She's the one who stole her!"

"Now, Jack," Mrs. Barker said quickly, "that's not nice."

"But, Mom—" Jack spluttered. Mrs. Barker rested a hand firmly on his shoulder—the "hand of doom," their father called it, because it meant that she didn't intend to say something sharp in front of guests, but nonetheless, you were to stop whatever you were doing immediately—and continued to smile at the girl. "Josie likes to wander around the neighborhood. I hope she wasn't bothering you."

"Oh, no," said the girl. "She comes over to my house a lot. I like her."

"And where do you live?" Mrs. Barker asked.

The girl pointed down the street. "It's a gray house. On Waltz Street."

"Well, it's very nice to meet you. I'm Ellen Barker, and these are my sons . . . Jack, Simon, and Henry. What's your name?"

The girl hesitated, looking at Josie. "Delilah Dunworthy," she said, a little shyly.

Henry exchanged a skeptical glance with Simon. What kind of name was that?

"Would you like to come inside?" Mrs. Barker asked. "Do you want something to drink? It's so hot here—that's the thing I can't seem to get used to. Oh, and before I forget, let me get your reward."

"Reward!" Simon cried. "That's ridiculous. She took Josie."

"Yeah," Henry complained. "She wouldn't give her back."

"I don't know what you boys are talking about," Mrs. Barker said sharply, and she looked at Henry the way she did whenever she said he was on thin ice, which was the verbal equivalent of the hand of doom.

She beckoned Delilah into the kitchen. "Is twenty dollars all right?" she asked, unsnapping her billfold. "Does that sound like a good reward?"

Twenty dollars! Henry smacked his forehead. This was unbelievable.

Delilah nodded. "Oh, yes! That's a lot."

Jack looked ready to explode. "Mom, you can't—"

But Mrs. Barker hushed him with another disapproving glance while she poured a glass of lemonade. "Here, Delilah, and how about a chocolate chip cookie?" She filled a plate and set it on the table.

Henry looked at Simon and Jack in disbelief. How could their mother give twenty dollars AND chocolate chip cookies to the girl who kidnapped Josie? It was outrageous.

Mrs. Barker continued talking to Delilah. "What grade are you going into?"

"Fifth," she said, smiling at the boys smugly. She sat down at the table and took a swig of lemonade, smacking her lips.

"Henry's in the same grade!" Mrs. Barker said.

Delilah turned to Henry. "Really? I thought you were younger than me."

Henry scowled at her.

"Maybe you'll be in the same class," Mrs. Barker continued.

"Maybe," Delilah said neutrally.

Mrs. Barker pushed the cookie plate in front of her and gave her a paper napkin. "Now, how long have you and your family lived in this area?"

"We're new," Delilah said. "We moved here in March."

"You did?" Mrs. Barker exclaimed. "We just moved here too!" She turned to the boys and widened her eyes slightly, a look that appeared to mean "see, you have so much in common" or "stop the nonsense about the cat right now and make friends with this girl."

Henry, Simon, and Jack huddled at one end of the table, fuming.

"Have you met other children in the neighborhood?" Mrs. Barker kept on talking.

"Some," Delilah said, "but lots of people are away on vacation."

She bit into a cookie. When Mrs. Barker turned away

to refill her glass of lemonade, Delilah made a face at the boys. "Yum! These cookies are dee-licious."

Henry couldn't stand it anymore. He grabbed his mother's arm. "You can't feed her! That's not fair! She took Josie and tried to pretend she was hers. She called her *Princess*!"

As if any normal person would name a cat Princess, Henry thought. Surely now their mother would understand.

"Henry, hush," Mrs. Barker said firmly. "You saw for yourself, Delilah brought Josie back home. You boys should thank her."

Henry, Jack, and Simon gaped in astonishment.

"That's it," Simon said. "We're going outside." He beckoned for Henry and Jack to follow him onto the deck before their mother could stop them.

They ran over to the swing set, as far away from the house as possible. It was their swing set from Chicago, painstakingly reconstructed here in Arizona by their father during the first two weekends after the move. Mrs. Barker had complained that he was doing that instead of helping her unpack, but Mr. Barker pointed out that there was nothing about Uncle Hank's house that made it seem like a place for kids, so the swing set was important.

Henry was grateful for it—in this strange desert place, it was the one thing that reminded him of their yard back home. Simon sat on a rung of the ladder that led to the fort, and Jack lay on his stomach on the slide. Henry plopped down on a swing and twisted around several times. "Mom is crazy."

The other two nodded glumly.

"How come she believed her?" Jack demanded.

"That girl is a tricky one," Henry observed.

The sliding door squeaked open, and Mrs. Barker came out with the plate of cookies. "What on earth is the matter with you boys?" she said.

"Where is she?" Henry asked suspiciously.

"Delilah? She went home. You didn't exactly make her feel welcome. What a nice girl. And you know how hard it is to be new in town. Especially a small town like Superstition, where everyone knows everyone else. You could have made a new friend."

"Mom," Simon said, rolling his eyes, "we don't need friends like that."

"Yeah," Jack boomed. "She stole Josie and locked her up—"

Mrs. Barker sighed. "I know it seemed that way to you, but it was just a misunderstanding. Delilah thought Josie was lost. And she brought her back home. It was very responsible of her. Besides, aren't you glad we have Josie back safe and sound? I was so worried she was lost on the mountain."

Henry peered up at her. "You were? But you kept saying she was fine."

"Well," Mrs. Barker allowed, "I was pretty sure she'd

be okay. But I was still worried. I just didn't want to alarm you boys."

"Why *were* you so worried?" Simon asked. Henry knew he was thinking of the strange glances between their parents and the policeman the night Josie went missing.

"Yeah," Jack chimed in, pushing up on his arms to stare at Mrs. Barker. "Did you think she would get eaten?"

Mrs. Barker paused. "No, not really. But you remember what Officer Myers said. Superstition Mountain is dangerous."

"That's what he said," Simon persisted, "but he didn't tell us why."

Mrs. Barker pursed her lips, abruptly finished with the conversation. "You could get lost or hurt. It's no place for children. I don't want you three going anywhere near the mountain. Do you understand?"

"But—" Henry began.

"Henry! I mean it." She turned back toward the house. "Let's just be grateful Josie is home again. And I hope you'll be nicer to Delilah in the future."

Henry groaned inwardly, but only inwardly because he didn't want another rebuke from his mother.

As soon as she was safely out of earshot, Simon stood up. "She's definitely keeping something from us," he said. "They all are. Something happened on the mountain they don't want to talk about."

"I know," Henry mumbled. "Do you think it has anything to do with"—he lowered his voice—"the skulls we found?"

"Those old bones?" Jack asked.

"Shhh," Simon hushed him. "Keep your voice down."

"But who do you think they belonged to? When they were alive, I mean," Jack asked. He swiveled around on the slide, and shot to the bottom, landing on the dry grass with a bump. "Ow!" He rubbed his backside.

This yard was nothing like the one at their old house in Illinois, which had been lush and green, soft as a carpet. Henry spun slowly on the swing, stirring up clouds of dust with his sneakers. He thought of the strange white skulls and the feeling in the canyon . . . tense and quiet, as if something bad were about to happen. "How can we find out what the *real* story is?" he wondered.

Simon rubbed his hand over his hair, making the spikes stand on alert, ready for action. "Let's go to the library," he said finally.

"The library?" Jack complained. "It's too quiet there."

"Well, we can't use the computer," Simon pointed out. "Mom won't let us be on it for that long, and if she catches us snooping around for stuff about the mountain, we'll get in trouble."

Henry nodded. Their mother had very strict rules about computer use. Simon continued, "The library should have old newspapers. And if something really bad happened on Superstition Mountain, somebody must have written about it."

Henry jumped off the swing. Simon was brilliant. "That's a great idea!" he said, grabbing Jack's hand and pulling him up from the ground.

"But don't tell Mom," Simon insisted, looking at Jack. "Really, Jack, don't mess up, okay? If you want to come with us, you have to show us we can trust you."

Jack's face scrunched indignantly. "I don't ever tell them anything!"

"Oh, yeah? What about on Mother's Day, when we got Mom the surprise—"

Henry intervened. "Come on, he won't tell. Let's just go before Mom says it's too close to dinner."

They quickly got permission from Mrs. Barker. "The

library? Now that's a good way to spend the afternoon—
we live so close to it. But be careful on your bikes and
make sure to watch Jack." After stuffing a few cookies in
their pockets for the trip, they rode off to find out what
had happened on Superstition Mountain.

CHAPTER 9

AT THE LIBRARY

As they approached Coronado Road, they rode past Delilah's gray house. She was sitting on the front steps, between the bright beds of flowers, looking bored. When she saw them, she immediately bounced to her feet and ran across the yard.

"Where are you going?" she called.

"None of your business," Simon said, zooming past.

"Yeah," Henry echoed. Hadn't she interfered with their lives enough?

"Cat stealer!" Jack shouted.

Delilah ran along the sidewalk, following them. "I did not steal your cat!" she yelled. "I told you, she comes over to my house all the time. Maybe she doesn't like you anymore."

"Josie loves us!" Jack yelled back.

"Well, she likes me better," Delilah answered, panting.

"Does not!"

"Does too!"

Jack's bike screeched to a halt, and he flung himself at Delilah. She deftly stepped out of the way, while he tumbled onto the grass.

"Jack!" Henry told him. "Cut it out. We don't have time for that."

"So where are you going?" Delilah cautiously helped Jack up, holding him at arm's length so he couldn't slug her.

"Let me go!" Jack squirmed.

"Just tell me where you're going," Delilah said.

Henry dragged Jack over to his fallen bike. "The library," he said curtly. "Now leave us alone."

Simon was three houses ahead, with his bike turned sideways, waiting for them. "Henry! Jack! Come ON."

They pedaled fast to catch up. Henry glanced over his shoulder, just once, to see what Delilah was doing. She was standing where they'd left her, brown braids hanging on either side of her freckled face, watching them ride away.

The library was a sprawling concrete building on one end of Coronado Road, the main avenue through town.

The boys slid their bikes into the rack at the edge of the parking lot and ran up the steps through the double doors. Inside, the building was bright and sunny, thanks to large glass windows across one end. Through them, Henry could see the sharp outline of Superstition Mountain. It filled the room.

At the circulation desk, a dark-haired woman was arranging books on a cart. She looked up when they entered and gave them a tight smile. Her hair was jet-black, which made her look young from a distance, but the skin of her face was leathery brown and wrinkled. Her eyebrows were thin, arched lines, as if they'd been drawn on with ink. Henry thought her mouth seemed as stiff and frozen as a doll's.

"Hello, children," she said in a syrupy voice. "How are you today?"

"Fine," Henry answered politely.

"Can I help you with something?"

"Yes." Simon strode up to the desk. "Could you tell us where the old newspapers are?"

"Of course. I'll show you." She walked past them, beckoning. "The recent issues are over here, in the periodicals area . . . going back about six months."

They trailed behind her to a carpeted area in the

corner of the library, surrounded by tall wooden shelves. The upper ones were arrayed with glossy magazines; the lower ones held stacks of newspapers.

"Is there something you're looking for?" The librarian fixed her bright eyes and persistent smile on Henry.

Henry shifted from one foot to the other. "Not really . . ."

"We want to learn more about the town," Simon blurted. "We just moved here."

Henry thought the librarian's gaze sharpened, but her mouth stayed exactly the same. That's what was so strange, he realized. The expression on her mouth didn't match her eyes.

"I thought you must be new. I didn't recognize you. Let me know if I can help you find anything. We have lots of wonderful books for boys your age," she said pleasantly, and went back to her desk.

"She's creepy," Jack said.

A man at one of the nearby tables glanced at them. He had round wire-rimmed glasses, and Henry thought he looked smart and serious, like a high school teacher.

"Shhh, Jack," Simon warned. "The librarian will hear you." He sat cross-legged in front of the shelves, and Henry and Jack squatted beside him.

Jack asked loudly, "What are we looking for?"

The man at the table sighed and closed his computer.

Simon glared at Jack. "You have to WHISPER. It's a library."

"Okay," Jack said, but Henry knew Jack's whisper was as loud as most people's regular voices. And the library was so quiet that even small sounds were forcefully distinct—the whirr of the air conditioner, the faint tap of computer keyboards, the creak of shifting chairs.

Simon handed them each a stack of newspapers, which they carried over to an empty table. Henry spread the first one out in front of him. Large black letters blared across the masthead: SUPERSTITION SENTINEL.

"What's a sentinel?" he asked Simon.

Simon shrugged. "Just some goofy name for a newspaper."

The man began gathering his things, which included large rolls of paper that looked like blueprints. "It means a lookout," he said. "Or a watchman."

"Like a guard?" Henry asked.

The man nodded.

"See, Jack," Simon said softly. "He's leaving because you were too loud."

Jack frowned, but the man shook his head in their direction. "No, that's not it. The internet's down again."

"Oh," Simon said. "That happens all the time at our house." It was one of the peculiarities of their new home that the internet frequently went out, as did the phone service, as did the electricity. "We might as well be living on the frontier," Mrs. Barker said, when she tried to e-mail something to one of her editors and it wouldn't go through.

Jack clambered up on a chair to lean over the newspaper. "What are we looking for?" he demanded.

"Something bad that happened on the mountain," Henry said.

"You won't find it there," the man said, hoisting his computer bag over one shoulder.

The boys looked up, startled.

"You should check out the local history area." As he walked away, he gestured to a low bookshelf across the room, beneath a colorful map of Arizona.

"Thanks," Henry said shyly, though he wondered . . . how could the man be so sure there was nothing in the papers?

When the man was out of earshot, Simon returned to the newspapers. "He doesn't know what we're looking for. Let's go through these first."

Of everything about Simon, it was the thing Henry most envied, how he was always certain he knew best, even when adults disagreed. It had less to do with being smart than being sure, Henry thought, wishing he were more that way himself.

They began leafing through the newspapers, pages crackling noisily.

"I can't read this," Jack announced.

"That's because you can't read," Simon said.

"I *can* read." Jack glowered at him. "I can't read *this*. The letters are too small, and it's got too many big words."

"I'll help you," said a familiar voice.

CHAPTER 10
THE MISSING

THEY TURNED TO SEE DELILAH standing by the shelves watching them.

"You followed us," Simon said accusingly.

"No, I didn't."

"Then what are you doing here?"

"I just felt like coming to the library," Delilah said nonchalantly. She pulled up a chair next to Jack's. "Here," she said. "That says 'Pioneer Days Draw Big Crowd.'"

"He doesn't need your help," Henry said. "Jack, just read the headlines. If anything important happened, it'll be in big letters."

"Look!" said Jack. "It's a picture of the parade."

The top newspaper on Jack's pile had a grainy black-and-white picture of the Pioneer Days Parade. Delilah's ribbon-festooned bike was nowhere to be seen, thank goodness.

"What are you looking for?" Delilah asked.

Henry and Simon exchanged beleaguered glances. "Nothing," they said simultaneously.

"Just tell me. I'll look too."

Henry hesitated. There were too many newspapers to cover by themselves, especially with Jack not able to read very well. He glanced at Simon. "It would go faster. . . ."

"Yeah," Delilah echoed.

Simon relented. "Okay, you can go through Jack's pile with him. We're looking for stories about Superstition Mountain. About anything bad that happened up there."

Delilah scooted her chair closer to the table and gamely sifted through the pages. "Why do you think something bad happened on the mountain?" she asked.

Henry slid over to make more room for her. "Well, are you allowed to go up there?"

Delilah considered. "No. When my mom's at work, I'm not supposed to go anywhere outside the neighborhood. She's afraid I'll get lost. Or somebody will take me."

Simon snorted. "Are you kidding? Nobody is going

to take you." Delilah scowled at him, but he continued casually, "Is your mom at work right now?"

She nodded, turning newspaper pages.

"Aha!" Simon crowed. "When we were at your house, you said she was *napping*."

"That was this morning," Delilah said calmly.

Henry studied her. "So she really was napping?"

"No," Delilah replied, unperturbed. "She was at work."

Jack jumped to his feet on the chair and thrust his finger in her face, shouting, "You lied!"

"Shhh, Jack," Henry and Simon both hissed at once.

"No, I didn't," Delilah said evenly. "My mom might have been napping *at work*. Her job is really boring. And anyway, I'm not supposed to tell strangers I'm home alone."

Henry shot a defeated look at Simon. This girl had an answer for everything. But he was mildly interested in the idea of Delilah being left home on her own. Mr. and Mrs. Barker claimed that even Simon was too young for that yet. Another kid's family was like a whole other civilization, Henry often thought—different rules and habits, different snacks that were allowed or forbidden, different bedtimes and acceptable television shows.

"Well, you are still a LIAR," Jack declared, undeterred,

and Henry felt glad, in this case, that it was impossible to reason with him.

Delilah ignored him. She shuffled through the papers as he leaned over her, peppering her with deafening whispers, "What does that say?" "What's that one?"

After a few minutes, she sat back in her chair and said, "It's a boring town. Nothing happens here. This is a waste of time."

"Yeah," Jack agreed.

Henry sighed. "It's all little stuff—the school's having a concert . . . somebody won a contest . . . a road's closed. There are a lot of power outages, and the fire department is always being called."

"Okay," Simon agreed, standing up. "I don't see anything either. Let's look in the local history area, like that guy said."

They wandered over to the section marked "Arizona History" and crouched in front of the bookshelf labeled "Superstition and Its Surrounds." It was crammed with fat, worn volumes. They smelled musty, like somebody's attic. Simon pulled out a book and showed them the cover: *Legends of Superstition Mountain.* "Take out anything that looks like it would tell us about the mountain," he directed.

So Henry and Delilah began sorting through the

shelves, while Jack stood on tiptoe, looking at the map of Arizona. Simon quickly assembled a pile of books at his feet. After a few minutes, Delilah sat cross-legged on the carpet with a stack of her own, including the book of legends that Simon had chosen.

"I'll see what's in here," she said.

Henry continued to scan the shelves. There were books about the Old West, about cowboys and outlaws, and about the Apache Indians. He thought about Uncle Hank crossing the plains as a scout for the U.S. Cavalry. He didn't see anything specifically about Superstition Mountain, but any of these books might mention the mountain, he supposed. He found a book called *Ghost Towns of the Old West.* "Hey," he said, showing it to Simon. "I wonder if the ghost town that policeman was talking about is in here."

"What ghost town?" Delilah wanted to know.

"It doesn't have real ghosts, silly," Jack told her condescendingly.

"Some abandoned frontier town that's near here," Simon said. "We're going to explore it sometime."

Henry glanced at him, surprised. That was exactly what they *weren't* supposed to do. The summer was sounding more and more interesting.

"Really?" Delilah's raised her eyebrows.

"Girls can't come," Jack declared. He flopped onto his stomach on the carpet. "These books are too long. We can never in a million years read all of them."

As much as Henry loved to read, he felt discouraged himself. They *were* long, with tiny type, and most of them didn't have pictures. And there were so many! Did Simon really mean they had to look through every book? He tried to find a short one for Jack. At the end of the bottom shelf was a cluster of thin pamphlets, held in place by a metal bracket. These were *very* short, Henry thought, cheered. But they seemed to be tourist brochures. They were covered with colorful photos advertising various attractions in the area: horseback riding, an old mining town, rafting on the Verde River. Wedged at one end was a thin white booklet, stapled down the middle, with black type on the front.

"Jack," he said, "take a little one instead. Here's a really short one—"

Henry stopped. The title read *Missing on Superstition Mountain: A faithful record of disappearances since 1880, compiled by the Superstition Historical Society.*

"Hey!" Henry waved the booklet under Delilah's nose. "Look at this! Simon, look!"

Delilah scrambled to her knees. "Ooooh . . ."

Simon crowded next to them. "Read what it says."

Henry dropped to the carpet and flattened the booklet open with one palm. "Huh," he said. "It's mostly a list."

"What kind of list?" Simon asked.

"Yeah," Jack clamored, propping himself up on an elbow. "Read it!"

"Okay. . . ." Henry started reading from the top of the first page: " 'Superstition Mountain has long been known as a site of unusual disappearances and deaths. In the interest of preserving our town's history and heritage, and as a resource for those who are considering exploring this area, the Superstition Historical Society offers this record of disappearances, accidental deaths, and suspected murders on the mountain from 1880 to the present.' "

Henry felt a chill slice through him. Simon, Jack, and Delilah stared.

"Murder?" Delilah asked. "Nobody said anything about murder."

"Nobody said anything about anything," Simon said. "No wonder Mom and Dad won't talk about it."

Henry read slowly, " '1880 . . . two soldiers found shot in the head. 1881 . . . prospector found dead after mine cave-in.' "

"What kind of mine?" Simon asked.

"It doesn't say. It's just a list." Henry leaned over the tiny type. "'1896 . . . Elisha Reavis, the Madman of Superstition Mountain, found de'"—he had to sound out the word—"'cap-it-ated.'"

"Decapitated?" Delilah repeated. She wrinkled her nose. "Yuck."

"What's decapitated?" Jack wanted to know.

"When somebody chops your head off." Delilah whacked the heel of her hand against his neck to illustrate.

Henry glanced at her in surprise. It was a word he hadn't heard before.

"Ewww," Jack said, simultaneously grossed out and impressed.

"I wonder why he was called the Madman of Superstition Mountain," Delilah said.

"Shhh, you guys," Simon scolded. "Keep reading, Hen."

Henry took a deep breath. "'1910 . . . unidentified woman's body found in cave near Weaver's Needle—'"

"Hey, that's the pointy rock," Jack noted.

"Listen," Henry insisted. "'Cause of death unknown. 1931 . . . disappearance of federal employee Adolph

Ruth . . .' oh!" Henry gasped. "It says his *skull* was found on Black Top Mountain with two bullet holes in it."

"Hey," Jack cried, "like when we found the three—"

Simon glared at Jack, while Henry shook his head quickly. Delilah knew nothing about the skulls. Jack stopped, his cheeks turning bright red. "Um," he said.

"The three what?" Delilah looked at him curiously.

"Nothing," Jack said.

Henry turned the page. "'1936 . . . body of Roman O'Hal of New York City found, cause of death: fall from cliff. 1937 . . . body of Guy Frink found, cause of death: gunshot wound to stomach. 1947 . . . body of James Cravey recovered in La Barge Canyon—'" Henry squinted at the small print. "'Decapitated.'"

"Another one?" Delilah raised her eyebrows.

Henry nodded uncomfortably. No wonder the mountain was off-limits! So many people had died there. He got to the bottom of the page and read, "1949," then looked up, puzzled, and held out the book for them to see.

"Hey . . . that's weird. The next page is torn out."

CHAPTER 11
ASKING FOR TROUBLE

THEY ALL STARED at the tattered edge of the paper.

"Just that one page is gone?" Simon asked. "What does the rest say?"

Henry turned the booklet around to show them. "It's a list of the Superstition Historical Society members. See? *Emmett Trask, President.*"

They sat in silence for a minute.

"Wow," Jack said. "That's a lot of people dead!"

"Or missing," Delilah added.

"No kidding," Simon said. "That's why our parents are acting so strange about the mountain." He took the booklet from Henry and leapt to his feet. "We should take this home with us. I'll check it out."

A few minutes later, he came back with the black-haired librarian.

"I'm sorry, this one doesn't circulate," the librarian said firmly, but in her same nicey-nice voice. "It's part of our reference collection."

"But it doesn't have a label," Simon protested. "And look, it's not even a whole book. Somebody tore out a page."

"Well, that's a shame, isn't it?" the librarian said. "It ruins the book for other patrons. I'll take it back to the office and see if it can be repaired." She held out her hand for the booklet, which Simon reluctantly gave her.

She turned to leave, but then looked back at them thoughtfully. "I'm Mrs. Thomas, the library director. What are your names?"

"Simon," Simon answered quickly. "This is Henry, and he's Jack."

"It's very nice to meet you." She extended her hand to each of them in turn. Henry took it awkwardly, noticing that it was cool and bony, and her fingertip was smudged black with ink. "What grades are you in?" Henry felt the familiar flood of panic that overcame him whenever a stranger was about to make a wrong assumption about his size or his age.

Simon jumped in quickly, "I'm going into sixth, Henry's going into fifth, and Jack will be in first."

"Oh," Mrs. Thomas said, her skinny eyebrows arching in surprise. "I thought—"

"And this is Delilah," Simon continued smoothly. Henry glanced at him gratefully.

"Your sister?" the librarian asked, turning to Delilah.

"No!" the boys chorused.

Delilah only smiled sweetly at Mrs. Thomas. "I'm Delilah Dunworthy."

"What a pretty name," Mrs. Thomas said. "Why don't you tell me what you're looking for? Perhaps I can help."

Henry wasn't sure. What if she reacted like their parents had? Maybe there was some big grown-up conspiracy to keep quiet about Superstition Mountain, the way grown-ups would never tell you all the bad stuff they did as kids because they were afraid you'd try it yourself. On the other hand, she did work here in the library, and it was her job to help people find out what they needed to know. Simon seemed to be making the same mental calculation.

Henry cleared his throat. "We . . . we wanted to know more about the mountain. If anything interesting has happened up there."

Mrs. Thomas's keen eyes fixed on his. "Things have been happening on that mountain for hundreds of years," she said. "It is not a place for children."

"Why not?" Jack piped up. "What kinds of things?"

Mrs. Thomas continued smiling, but her eyes hardened.

"Bad things," she said.

When she said nothing more, the silence seemed to expand uncomfortably. Finally, Delilah asked, "Are there other books besides this one that we could check out?"

The librarian's forehead furrowed. "None of the books on this bottom shelf circulate. But you can check out anything from the upper shelves . . . that volume of legends, for instance." She motioned to the one Delilah had been reading earlier. "Just bring them to the circulation desk when you're ready." She gave them a final piercing look of appraisal, then walked away.

Henry eyed the booklet tucked under her arm longingly. He chose a book on the history of Arizona from the top shelf. Delilah picked up the book of legends.

"That was weird, huh?" Delilah said. "She wouldn't tell us anything."

"Probably because those people died in a really gross, bloody way," Simon speculated. "Grown-ups never want to talk about that."

This was particularly true of Mr. Barker, Henry thought. It was well-known family lore that he had fainted when Simon was born and was barred from the labor and delivery room ever after. He looked sick to his stomach whenever the boys mentioned any number of fascinating topics, like the size of a hairball Josie threw up or the way their cousin Brendan's finger bent sideways when he fell off his scooter. Mrs. Barker, on the other hand, could be counted on to show the appropriate level of curiosity about even the most grotesque physical condition or injury, because she usually had had to illustrate something similar at some point in her career.

"Yeah," Henry agreed. "And it sounds like a lot of people are still missing. Superstition Mountain is kind of like the Bermuda Triangle, except on land."

"What triangle?" Jack asked.

"It's a place in the ocean where planes and ships disappear," Henry told him. "They fly through this one area, and then, nobody knows why, but they lose all radio contact and are never heard from again. The other name for it is the Devil's Triangle."

"Well," Simon amended, "not *all* the planes and ships that pass through there disappear . . . just a few of them. And lots of people think there's a normal explanation. Like whirlpools or storms. Things like that."

"Probably there are a bunch of wrecks at the bottom of the ocean in that exact spot," Delilah said.

"Nope," Henry told her. "Whole entire ships and planes have disappeared without a trace."

"Well, that's freaky." Delilah twisted one braid. "But everyone's heard of the Bermuda Triangle, and nobody talks about Superstition Mountain that way. If people disappear up there all the time, why haven't we heard about it?"

Henry couldn't think of a good answer for this, but Simon said, "Maybe it does happen all the time, or at least a lot, but the grown-ups are keeping it quiet because they don't want to scare us."

They carried their two books to the circulation desk, where Mrs. Thomas was waiting for them.

"Now, who has a library card?" she asked.

The boys looked at one another in surprise—they'd been to the library several times, but their mother had always been the one to check things out—when Delilah pulled a small plastic card from her pocket.

"I do," she said, sliding it across the counter, to the boys' relief.

Mrs. Thomas pushed the two books toward Henry. "It was nice to meet all of you. Delilah Dunworthy . . . Simon, Jack, and . . . Henry, was it? Henry what? What's your last name, dear?"

Henry felt oddly hesitant to tell her, but there didn't seem to be a good reason not to. "Barker," he answered, reaching for the books.

Her eyes widened, and her hand tightened over the books so that Henry couldn't budge them. "Barker? Didn't you move into Hank Cormody's house?"

"How do you know that?" Jack exclaimed. "He's our great-uncle!"

"Was he?" Mrs. Thomas gazed at them so intently it made Henry squirm. He wanted to pick up the books, but with her hand resting on them like that, he thought it might seem like he was trying to snatch them away. He briefly imagined wrestling her for them.

"I should have known that's who you were," the librarian said, almost to herself. "Barker."

"We really need to go," Simon interrupted. "Our mom will wonder what's taking us so long."

"Of course." She reluctantly released the books, and

Henry hugged them to his chest. "Welcome to Superstition! I hope you'll use the library often. And about the mountain . . . remember what I said."

"We will," Simon answered. He led the way through the double doors into the library parking lot, which blazed in the afternoon sun.

CHAPTER 12
THE SUPERSTITION HISTORICAL SOCIETY

"WHY WAS SHE so interested in your uncle?" Delilah asked, as soon as they had pedaled a short distance down the street.

She had both library books balanced in the wicker basket of her bike. It looked like the same goofy bike she'd ridden in that parade, Henry thought. But at least it didn't have all the ribbons tied to it.

"Well," Henry began, "Uncle Hank was *eccentric*. He was a scout for the U.S. Cavalry and a cowboy and got into fistfights—"

"And he even killed a rattlesnake with a screwdriver once!" Jack interrupted.

Henry paused. "I'm named after him," he finished modestly.

"You are?" Delilah seemed impressed.

"Yeah," Henry said, pleased.

"But your name is Henry."

"Henry was his real name. Hank is the nickname for Henry," Henry told her, but it didn't seem very plausible even to him.

"That doesn't sound right," Delilah said.

Henry sighed and rode up alongside Simon. "It was weird that librarian knew who we were as soon as she heard our last name, didn't you think?" he asked.

Simon considered. "Yeah. But it's a small town. It seems like everybody knows everybody else. And Dad always said Uncle Hank was a character, so people would remember him."

"I wish we could have checked out that little book," Henry said.

"Me too!" Jack yelled, speeding past them. "That had all the good stuff in it."

Simon turned his wheel abruptly toward the curb and stopped, while they all squealed to a halt around him. "Wait a second—it was something that the historical society did, right? Maybe we can get a copy straight from them."

"That's a great idea!" Henry exclaimed.

"We just need an address. Let's ride over to Dad's and see if he has a phone book."

"I'll go first," Jack said, zooming off.

"Hold on!" Simon pedaled furiously after him. "Mom doesn't want you crossing the streets without me."

Henry started to follow, but then realized Delilah was still at the curb, awkwardly rotating her bike in the opposite direction.

"What are you doing?" he asked.

"Going home," she said. Her cheeks were pink, which made the freckles stand out even more. Henry thought she seemed upset.

"Why?"

"Well, you're going to your dad's," Delilah said.

"Aren't you coming?"

She looked at him. "Can I?"

Henry blinked. Girls were so weird. "Don't you want to?"

"Yes," she said.

Henry rode off, calling to her, "Then come on!"

When they reached their father's masonry shop, he was standing outside talking to a customer. He smiled when he saw them. "What's up, guys?"

"Do you have a phone book?" Simon asked. "We need an address."

"Sure, in the office," Mr. Barker replied. "Who's your friend?"

"She's just following us around," Jack said promptly.

Henry glanced at Delilah, who shifted on her bike. "This is Delilah," he said to his father. "She lives by us."

"Oh!" Mr. Barker said, his grin broadening. "The girl who found our long-lost cat! It's a pleasure to meet you. We certainly appreciate your help getting Josie back."

The boys groaned, but their father stretched out his hand. Delilah shook it, glancing at the boys smugly. "That's okay," she said politely. "I'm glad I found her."

Henry rolled his eyes at Simon, then led the way into the reception area. A yellow phone book sat on the desk. He thumbed through the pages, looking for a Superstition Historical Society listing.

"There's nothing here," he said finally. "Do you think it could be called something else?"

Simon thought. "Maybe just 'historical society'?"

Henry flipped backward to the *H*'s. Simon, Delilah, and Jack huddled over the page, scanning the columns of names.

"Is it there?" Jack demanded.

The names went from someone named Hipley to someone named Hiverton. Henry closed the book dejectedly.

"So now what?" he asked.

"I have an idea," Delilah said, twirling one braid.

Simon shot her a skeptical look. "What?"

"Why don't we look for that guy who was the president. Emmett something. Remember? You said his name, Henry. He'd probably have a copy of the book."

"Emmett Trask!" Henry exclaimed. He flipped quickly to the last chunk of pages, running his index finger down the list of *T* last names. "Trask! Here it is. And it has his address—44 Black Top Mesa."

"Dad!" Simon yelled. "Do you have a map?"

"A map of what?" Mr. Barker answered.

"Superstition! Superstition! Superstition!" Jack shouted. "We're trying to find someplace. It's important!"

"In the top desk drawer," came their father's faint reply.

Simon spread the map across the desk and checked the index. "Okay, here it is," he said finally, tracing his finger along a thin, curving black line. "This little crooked road past the cemetery."

"That's almost out of town," Delilah said. "Can we ride there on our bikes?"

"Sure," Simon scoffed. "This town is tiny. It's not far."

Henry thought their mom might have a different opinion about the distance to the edge of town, but he said nothing. He wanted so badly to know what was on the missing page.

They clambered back onto their bikes. Their father, still immersed in conversation, glanced their way. "Where are you off to now?" he asked.

"We're—" Jack began.

"Just riding around," Simon interrupted. They raced off down the street before Mr. Barker could ask any more questions.

It took them almost half an hour to ride all the way to Black Top Mesa. Simon was right, the town was small, and it wasn't long before they reached the outskirts. But Black Top Mesa, as it happened, was not a paved road. It was dirt and gravel, full of ruts, and it threw up clouds of brown dust as they rode. Jack's front wheel kept twisting in potholes, causing him to tumble. Finally Henry hung back, riding in front of him to lead him safely around the worst ones. Superstition Mountain loomed ahead. Even in the daylight, it seemed menacing and full of shadows.

The number 44 was painted on a metal mailbox toward the end of the road. A long gravel drive led to a small white house with a red pickup truck parked next to it. Simon rode his bike partway down the driveway and stopped, facing the front door. The others followed.

"Okay, you guys, let me do the talking," he instructed them.

Delilah assessed the house. "I don't know," she said. "Do you think it's okay? I mean, he's a stranger."

Henry wavered. Their mother would certainly not think it was okay.

"You don't have to come if you're scared," Simon said impatiently.

"Yeah, we're not scared," Jack said.

Henry was a little scared. "I think it's okay if we stay together," he ventured. Before they could make up their minds, the door opened and a tall man wearing glasses stepped onto the porch.

"You guys need something?" he called to them. He looked at them more closely. "You're pretty far from the library."

"Oh!" Henry cried. "It's that guy! The one with the computer."

"He's not a stranger," Jack announced, promptly pedaling right up to the porch steps. Henry hesitated, then followed him, with Simon and Delilah close behind.

"Are you Emmett Trask?" Simon asked, as their four bikes skidded to a stop, spraying gravel.

He studied them curiously. "Yep, that's me. What can I do for you?"

"The president of the Superstition Historical Society?" Simon continued.

Emmett Trask raised his eyebrows. "Not anymore. Why?"

Henry slumped in disappointment.

"We came all this way for nothing!" Jack protested.

"What are you looking for?" Emmett asked. "I can give you the name of the new president. But you probably already met her."

Henry and Simon exchanged bewildered glances.

"Where?" Delilah asked.

"At the library. It's Julia Thomas, the director."

CHAPTER 13
MOUNTAIN MYSTERIES

HENRY SHUDDERED. The black-haired librarian! One thing seemed certain: *she* would never help them find the missing page.

"THAT lady?" Jack cried. "The creepy one?"

Emmett laughed.

"She wasn't very helpful," Delilah told him. "She took the book we wanted and wouldn't let us check it out. It was a book from the historical society."

"*Missing on Superstition Mountain*?" Emmett said. "I've got a copy."

"You do?" Simon asked. "Can we borrow it?"

"I'll give you one. I've got at least a dozen of them. That was the historical society's main research project while I was president. But first, tell me how you found me."

"We saw your name in the list of historical society

members and looked you up in the phone book," Henry said.

"So Julia didn't send you here? The librarian?"

Henry shook his head.

"Good," Emmett answered, leaning against the side of the house. "Why are you so interested in *Missing on Superstition Mountain*?"

When Simon paused, Henry jumped in. "We just moved here, and we're trying to find out more about the mountain." And then, because Emmett Trask didn't seem like a parent—didn't seem like he'd fuss and scold and pester them with warnings—"We're not allowed to go up there, but nobody will tell us why."

Emmett snorted. "I'll tell you."

They looked at him expectantly, and he took a breath, as if he weren't sure where to begin. "Well, there have been over twenty disappearances or deaths on the mountain. Which makes it not a safe place for anyone, let alone kids. Now, I'm sure there are rational explanations for what happened up there, but it's not always obvious what they are. . . ." Henry thought of the list in the book; the people missing and murdered. It certainly wasn't obvious to him what the rational explanation would be.

"What's 'rational'?" Jack asked.

"It means logical," Henry told him, and Emmett elaborated, "Within the bounds of human knowledge. Something that has a natural or human cause . . . not supernatural."

Henry doubted that Jack understood any of that, but he sat back on his bike seat, seeming satisfied.

Emmett continued, "But the thing is, some people around here don't like rational explanations. They'd rather have a supernatural one. So they say the mountain is haunted or cursed, under a spell." His mouth turned down in disgust. "That's why I left the historical society. Those folks aren't interested in historical research anymore. It's turned into a club for ghost hunters and treasure seekers."

Frankly, Henry thought ghost hunting and treasure seeking sounded much more interesting than historical research. What if there were ghosts on Superstition Mountain? He remembered the feeling of being watched, the prickles on the back of his neck.

"Treasure?" Simon asked, his face brightening. "What treasure?"

Emmett shook his head. "Oh, there probably isn't any. But the rumor is there's a gold mine, the Lost Dutchman's Mine, hidden somewhere on the mountain. It's supposed to be one of the richest veins of gold anywhere in the West. People have been searching the mountain for over a hundred years trying to find it."

A gold mine! Henry pictured the gold mines in movies and books, where people walked into a cave and discovered that the walls, floor, and ceiling were sparkling with precious gold.

"GOLD!" Jack cried, bouncing on the toes of his sneakers and almost falling off his bike. "Wow!"

Simon flashed Henry a quick glance, and asked Emmett, "Why do people think that?"

Emmett looked annoyed. "You know, if that's what you guys are interested in, you really should talk to the historical society. That's all they care about these days—figuring out the location of the Lost Dutchman's Mine."

"But it's gold!" Jack insisted. "If we found it, we'd be RICH."

"Yeah, that's the idea," Emmett said. "But people have been looking for that mine for over a century and haven't found anything. If you ask me, it's a big distraction from the real research we should be doing, about the Apaches and the early settlers . . . the Spanish influence in this area."

Which all sounded mind-numbingly boring compared to a hidden gold mine, Henry thought. Who wanted to learn about early settlers when you could be searching for the biggest pile of gold in the country?

Simon leaned over the front of his bike, not the least put off by Emmett's dismissive comments. "But *why* do they think there's a gold mine on the mountain? And whose gold is it?"

Emmett ran his hand through his hair. "There's no question that there's gold on the mountain. Plenty of people have found gold ore, starting with the Spanish in the 1500s. But it was pretty well tapped out in the 1800s;

I doubt there's anything left to speak of. As to who it belongs to . . . well, I guess you'd have to say it belonged to the Apaches originally. Or to the mountain. But as far as the Lost Dutchman's Mine, that belonged to Jacob Waltz."

"Waltz? That's the name of my street!" Delilah exclaimed.

"Most of the streets around here are named for historical people or places," Emmett told her. "Waltz wasn't a Dutchman—as a matter of fact, he was German. Came here in the mid-1800s. Supposedly, he and his partner discovered gold on Superstition Mountain and struck it rich. They kept the mine a secret, and after their deaths, nobody ever found it."

"And people have died looking?" Simon asked. "That's the big secret, the reason our parents won't let us go up the mountain?"

"Well, that and a few other things," Emmett replied.

What other things? Henry wondered. "How did people die?" he asked, but even as he said it, he realized that he knew the answer: they were shot, or fell into canyons, or had their heads cut off. That wasn't the important question. The important question was *why* did people die? Why was the mountain so dangerous a place that to climb it meant to risk your very life?

Jack blurted out, "Yeah, our mom says there are mountain lions and rattlesnakes! Did people get EATEN?"

Emmett shook his head. "There are mountain lions and rattlesnakes, but they haven't killed anyone lately, to my knowledge. Sometimes it's a rock slide. Or a flash flood that fills a canyon and drowns someone. There are a lot of steep slopes . . . people have fallen. But more often, they just get lost on the mountain without enough water. They die of dehydration."

Henry felt a tremor go through him, remembering their trip up the mountain and Jack falling into the hidden canyon where the three skulls perched.

Emmett sat down on the top step of the porch. He rubbed the bridge of his nose, dislodging his glasses, and for a moment, he looked not smart and earnest and teacherish, the way he had when they first saw him in the library, but vaguely goofy, like a big kid himself.

"And then there are the deaths that haven't been fully explained," he said. "People get worked up over those. That's why there's so much talk about the mountain being haunted." He seemed to be choosing his words carefully. "But the truth is, whenever there's a scarce, valuable resource—like gold—and a bunch of people wanting it, there are reasons to get rid of the competition."

Henry thought again of the long list of names in *Missing on Superstition Mountain,* each of them a real person whose life had ended unexpectedly. Violently. Too soon.

"You mean people have been murdered," Simon said, unfazed.

"Well, yes. Some have died of gunshot wounds. Some have been decapitated."

That word again. Delilah stiffened, and Henry pictured the bleached skulls. "Did they catch the people who did it?" he asked softly.

"No, not in most cases. This is rough, isolated country . . . lots of places to hide for someone who doesn't want to be found." Emmett smiled suddenly. "There used to be a fellow in Superstition who was a pro at hiding in the mountains. He made a lot of money gambling in the little towns around here, quite a cardplayer. When the people he beat at poker came looking for him to get their money back, he would hightail it into the mountains for weeks at a time. They never found him." His smile broadened. "So I guess you could say Superstition Mountain has saved a few lives too."

Henry shivered. He couldn't imagine anyone staying overnight on the mountain. He thought of how the wind would sound blowing through the canyons in the black night. "What happened to that guy?" he asked.

Emmett sighed. "He died a few months ago." Then, seeing their faces, "Don't worry, it wasn't anything suspicious. I don't know how old he was, but he'd led a long, full life. Used to be a scout for the cavalry, actually."

Henry gasped, and Simon interjected, "Wait a second—that's our uncle!"

CHAPTER 14

"THEY WEREN'T THE SAME . . ."

EMMETT STARED AT THEM. "Huh?"

"Hank Cormody! He's our uncle."

"Yeah," Jack added. "We just moved into his house."

Delilah turned to Henry in wonderment. "Everybody knows your uncle," she said. "The lady at the library, now this guy . . ."

Emmett was still looking confused. "Hank Cormody was your uncle? But you're way too young—"

"Well, he's our *great*-uncle," Simon amended. "But we're still related to him."

"And you're living in his house?"

Simon nodded. "We inherited it."

"Well, isn't that something! So you're Hank Cormody's family. It's funny, you know, because he pretty much kept to himself, but Hank was a legend around here."

Emmett stood up, swinging the door wide. "Here, why don't you come in? I'll get that booklet for you."

"Sure!" Jack said. His bike clattered to the ground, and he charged up the stoop past the others.

Delilah watched disapprovingly. "I'll wait here," she said primly.

Henry looked at Simon. They weren't allowed to go into a stranger's house, not ever. But it was worse to let Jack go by himself. And this guy did know their uncle . . . so he wasn't a total stranger. Simon seemed to have come to the same conclusion, because he hopped off his bike and climbed the steps of the porch two at a time. With a sheepish glance at Delilah, Henry followed.

The inside of Emmett Trask's house was dark and messy, in a way that made Henry immediately feel relaxed. Nobody would have to worry about tracking mud or leaving water rings on a table here. Two of the walls were lined with bookshelves, and the large wood table at one end of the living room held several teetering piles of books and papers. An enormous map hung over a desk in one corner. When Henry walked over for a closer look, he saw that it was a patchwork of pastel colors, covered with tiny lines and numbers.

"It's a geological survey map of this area." Emmett stood behind him. "Those numbers are the elevations: how high the land is at each point."

"Cool," Henry said, studying the cluster of wavy, numbered lines that marked the slopes of the mountain.

"Wow!" Jack cried from a distant room. "Look at all these ROCKS!"

Henry could hear Simon hiss something in rebuke.

"You found my office," Emmett said, unconcerned. Henry thought the living room looked like an office too, cluttered as it was with books and papers.

Jack emerged from a back hallway with Simon close behind him. "How come you have all those rocks?"

"It's what I do," Emmett said, pointing to the desk, where Henry noticed a shallow tray full of rocks. "I'm a geologist." He scanned the bookshelf and plucked a familiar-looking pale pamphlet from a batch at the end of a row of books. "Is this what you were looking for?" he asked, handing it to Henry.

"Yes!" Henry wanted to flip to the missing page, but he restrained himself. The booklet was crisp and new. "Thanks," he said, feeling shy.

"Yeah, thanks," Simon echoed, pushing Jack ahead of him. "We should head home. We've been riding around for hours."

They crowded onto the porch, where Delilah stood at the bottom with her bike leaning against her hip, looking both nervous and annoyed.

"It's time to go. We've been here too long," she said to Henry in an accusing voice.

"Yeah, I know," Henry agreed. "We're leaving now." He turned to Emmett with the pamphlet in his hand. "Does this have everything? All the people who've disappeared?"

Emmett hesitated. "It's as complete as we could make it. We went back and looked at the records from the late 1800s, though of course that time isn't well documented. So many of those disappearances aren't confirmed. But it's got pretty much everything, except . . ."

"Except what?" Delilah asked. She took the booklet from Henry and placed it in her basket with the library books.

"Well . . ." Emmett hesitated again. "There have been disappearances on the mountain that aren't recorded in the book, because the people were found eventually."

"Found alive?" Simon asked. "That doesn't count, then. It's not a disappearance if they turn up."

"Right," Emmett agreed. "That was my argument for not including them on the list. Although . . . well, they were found, but they weren't the same. They came back from the mountain changed."

CHAPTER 15

THE LAST PAGE

HENRY STARED AT HIM. "What do you mean?"

Emmett took a deep breath. "This stuff only feeds the rumors about the mountain. It's why your parents are so worried about you going anywhere near it."

"What stuff?" Simon demanded. "What are you talking about?"

Emmett rubbed his forehead. "Have you heard anything about Sara Delgado?"

They looked at him blankly.

"Do you know what a fugue state is?"

Henry thought *fugue* sounded like a cloud of smelly perfume.

"A fugue state is kind of a walking coma," Emmett told them. "In other words, the person is out of it, can't remember anything that's happened to them, doesn't know who or where they are, but is able to function normally otherwise."

"Like *amnesia*?" Henry asked. He once read a book about someone who got hit on the head and developed amnesia, forgetting everything about his former life.

"Yes, like that. Sara Delgado is a local girl, daughter of the caretaker at the cemetery. To be honest, I don't think she was all there to begin with; she was kind of spacey and hard to talk to. But, anyway, last summer, she went missing. Had a fight with her father and went up the mountain. She was gone for three days. A search party found her, scratches and bruises all over her body, terrified out of her mind. She was in a fugue state. She's never been able to remember what happened to her."

Henry shuddered. "That's spooky."

"Yeah," Jack whispered.

Delilah twirled one braid, saying nothing.

Simon pursed his lips, studying the booklet propped innocuously in Delilah's basket. "So you're saying she's not on the list? Which means that not every strange thing that's happened on the mountain is in the book."

"Exactly," Emmett said. "But the Sara Delgado thing is unexplained *right now*; that doesn't mean there isn't an explanation. We just don't have enough information to know what it is."

"Not everything has to have an explanation," Delilah snapped. "Some things just happen."

They all turned to her in surprise, and Simon said, "Sure, some things happen, but there's usually an explanation."

"It's time to go," Delilah repeated. "Our moms will be mad."

"Do you want to call home? You're welcome to use the phone." Emmett sounded apologetic. "I didn't mean to scare you guys."

"You didn't scare us," Simon said quickly. "And besides, I would rather know what's going on, even if it's scary. Nobody else would tell us anything."

That was how Simon was, Henry realized—he would always rather know the truth. Henry himself wasn't so sure. What were those two sayings? *Knowledge is power* and *Ignorance is bliss.* Which was more true? Henry wondered. Maybe it depended on what the knowledge was. In the case of Superstition Mountain, ignorance might be better. Henry was beginning to understand why their parents didn't want to talk about Superstition Mountain.

But at least Emmett Trask hadn't given them the usual grown-up runaround.

"Well, now you know. That's the reason your parents don't want you on the mountain," Emmett concluded. "Not because of ghosts or curses—just because it's a dangerous place. If you run into trouble up there, it's hard to get help."

"Yeah, it sounds like it," Simon said. "Thanks again for the book."

"Of course," said Emmett. "I'll see you guys around town, I'm sure. Maybe at the library." He smiled at them.

They climbed on their bikes, and Delilah organized the books, positioning them carefully in her basket. Then they rode down the gravel drive toward home.

It was almost evening by the time they reached their neighborhood, and they were all starving.

"We forgot to have lunch!" Jack cried, horrified.

"There wasn't time," Simon said. "And now dinner will be almost ready."

"I don't want dinner," Jack whined. "I want to have lunch."

"Well, it's too late. You can't go back and have lunch—you missed it."

Henry could see Jack's lower lip start to tremble. "You were supposed to take care of me," he complained. "You forgot to give me lunch!"

"We're not your babysitters," Simon snapped. "Unless you're a BABY."

"I want lunch *and* dinner."

"It's okay, Jack," Henry told him. "You can ask Mom for something when we get home." Privately, Henry thought it was unlikely that Mrs. Barker would give him anything before dinner (it was already five thirty), but the missed lunch was exactly the type of thing that upset Jack—something he was owed and felt cheated out of.

Delilah braked to a stop at the corner of her street. She took the Arizona history book from her basket and handed it to Henry, then gave him Emmett Trask's booklet.

"Tell me what it says, okay?" she said. "I wish we had time to read it now."

"Yeah, me too. But I'll look at it tonight and call you if there's anything interesting," Henry promised.

"Thanks." Delilah smiled at him. "My number is 555–3233. Can you remember that?"

Henry nodded. "The first three are the same as our number, and the last part is easy—3233."

"And I'll look at the book of legends," Delilah added.

"We should check for stuff on the computer too." She turned and rode away, her braids streaming over her shoulders.

"She was actually kind of useful," Simon commented. "At least more useful than I expected. Especially with the library card."

"Ugh!" Jack bellowed over his shoulder, racing ahead. "She's a GIRL!"

"Well," Henry said, "some girls are useful."

That night over dinner, the boys gave a much-abbreviated description of their day to their parents.

"But you were gone so long!" Mrs. Barker protested.

"You told us not to interrupt you," Simon answered coolly. "You said you needed to work."

"I did need to work, and I must admit, I got a lot done," Mrs. Barker answered. "But I didn't expect you to be gone all day! You didn't even come back for lunch."

Jack looked aggrieved all over again. "And I was *really* hungry," he complained.

Mrs. Barker rubbed the bridge of her nose and straightened her glasses. "Simon, I expect you to be the responsible one."

"I am the responsible one!" Simon exploded. "I

watched him when we crossed the streets. I kept an eye on him at the library. Next time I'm just going to leave him home."

Jack shot Henry a worried glance. "It's okay," he announced magnanimously. "I'm not hungry anymore. I ate my whole dinner."

Neither outburst fazed Mrs. Barker. "I just don't understand why you couldn't check in with me," she continued. "Do you mean to say you were riding around town the whole afternoon? I find that hard to believe."

"We did check in," Simon countered. "We checked in with Dad. We stopped at his office."

"Did they?" Their mother turned to their father in exasperation. "You could have told me."

"Yeah, Dad, you should have told her," Simon echoed.

"It's Dad's fault," Henry agreed.

"Now, hold on." Mr. Barker lifted his hands in front of his chest. "You guys came by for less than ten minutes. I seem to recall you raided my office for a map, then took off. Care to explain where you went?"

Henry and Simon exchanged glances. "We were just riding around," Henry said.

"With Delilah?" Mr. Barker turned to Mrs. Barker. "I met our illustrious cat finder."

"Isn't she cute?" Mrs. Barker smiled. "With all those freckles, she looks like someone dunked her in cinnamon."

Henry wrinkled his nose. Their mother had a habit of saying sappy things like that.

"No, she doesn't," Jack argued. "She's SPOTTED."

"Well, I think she's adorable," Mrs. Barker said. "And I'm glad you boys have at least one friend in the neighborhood now. She seems like a sweet girl."

Their mother often referred to girls this way: cute, sweet, adorable. Henry sometimes wondered if she wished she *had* a girl, instead of three boys. Or maybe in addition to three boys. Did she want someone who would dress in frilly outfits? Play with dolls? Or do any of the other innumerable, boring things that girls liked to do, like make up stories with their plastic horses, or fix each other's hair, or talk for hours about the silly things people said at school?

"Can we be excused?" Simon asked, in a tone that made it sound like an order. "To play outside before it's dark?"

"All right," Mrs. Barker decided. "But stay in the yard this time, okay? And, Simon . . ."

Simon, halfway out the sliding glass door, groaned.

"Honey, I mean it. Next time, you need to call and let

me know what's going on. I realize this is a new place and you're having fun exploring, but I need to know where you boys are. That you're all right."

"Okay, Mom!" They fled before she could think up any more rules for them.

Out in the dusky yard, Henry opened the crisp copy of *Missing on Superstition Mountain* and placed it on the tufted patch of grass between them, smoothing it flat. He turned to the page that had been torn from the booklet at the library.

"Okay, let's see what it says," he said to Simon and Jack.

"Yeah, what does it say?" Jack cried. "Read it!"

Henry cleared his throat. "The last one I read was 1947, right? The guy who was decapitated?"

"With no head!" Jack said enthusiastically.

"Jack, not so loud," Simon warned. "Do you want them to come out here and ask what we're talking about?"

"No," Jack whispered, chastened.

"Okay, listen," Henry began. " '1951 . . . body of Dr. John Burns found. Cause of death: gunshot wound to chest. 1952 . . . skeleton of Joseph Kelley found near Weaver's Needle—' "

"Again, it's by the landmark," Simon noted.

"Keep reading," Jack urged.

"Okay, okay," Henry said. " '1952 . . . skeleton of Joseph Kelley found near Weaver's Needle. Disappearance of—' " He stopped. His eyes widened.

"What?" Simon asked. "Disappearance of what?"

Henry lifted his head slowly, his finger pressed to the page like a dart stuck to a bull's-eye. " 'Disappearance of three Texas boys. Presumed dead; bodies never recovered.' "

CHAPTER 16
TELLING SOMEONE

Nobody said anything, not even Jack. To Henry, the silence was deafening.

Simon took the booklet from him and read the line to himself. His eyebrows knit together. "What should we do?"

Henry was so startled to be asked that by *Simon*, he could only stare at him.

Jack bounced forward on his knees. "It's the skulls!" he whispered fiercely. "We found them!"

"Well," Simon ventured, "it might not be those same boys. Just because we found the skulls together doesn't mean they belonged to people who were together on the mountain."

That could be true, Henry realized. But deep inside, he felt that it wasn't. "We should have brought them back with us," he said, turning to Simon. "I wanted to, remember? You said no."

Simon looked down at the page. "I didn't think it mattered. I mean, they'd been up there for such a long time! And I was right about that. You said the Texas boys went missing in 1952."

Henry bit his lip. He knew there was no point in blaming Simon. "Okay, okay. What do we do now?"

"Tell someone, I guess," Simon said reluctantly.

"Let's call Delilah."

"I meant a grown-up."

"Yeah," Jack said. "Why would we tell her? She doesn't know anything about those skulls."

Henry hesitated. "But she knows about the other stuff, and she's . . . she's part of it now."

"But—" Jack started to complain again, but Henry glared at him. "Okay," he said glumly. "You'll be sorry."

Simon shrugged. "Fine. I don't care—tell Delilah. But that doesn't solve the problem. I think we have to call the police. Those three guys have been missing for, like, sixty years."

Henry said slowly, "Their parents probably aren't even alive anymore." For some reason that seemed too sad to contemplate.

"What if their parents are alive and have wondered all this time what happened to them?" Simon asked softly. They were silent, staring at the page.

Jack sat back on his heels, looking worried. "What if we can't find the canyon again?"

This was a good point, Henry had to admit. What if they told the police, led them up the mountain, and then couldn't find the skulls? Nobody would believe them. And they'd have to admit they went up the mountain in the first place, which would cause all kinds of trouble with their parents.

Simon looked grim. "If we tell Mom and Dad we were on the mountain, they'll probably ground us for the rest of the summer."

Henry thought for a minute. "What if we go up the mountain again and get the skulls ourselves? We could bring them back here and . . . maybe we could say we found them in the desert?"

Simon frowned. "I don't know. That's probably the same as disturbing a crime scene." He wavered. "But it's been so long. I don't think that ledge where we found the skulls is where they died. There were no other bones there. And the skulls were lined up in a row."

"So what are we going to do?" Jack demanded. "We can't be grounded! That is so BORING."

"But if we go up there again . . ." Henry faltered. "What if something happens to us?"

He looked across the yard at the hulking shadow of the mountain, far in the distance. He thought of the tree branch crashing to the ground so close to him. His heart quickened. "Like whatever happened to that Sara Delgado girl that Emmett Trask told us about?"

"You mean the 'fugue state'? That sounded pretty bad," Simon agreed. He rubbed one hand over his hair. "I think we should go talk to her and see what we can find out. Then we can decide whether to get the skulls."

Henry felt a small wave of relief. It was beginning to seem like they had a plan.

"What else does it say in the book?" Simon asked. "How many more people are on that list?"

Henry smoothed the pages. The purplish dusk made it difficult to see the print.

"'1956 . . . body of unidentified man found, cause of death: gunshot wound to head. 1960 . . . skull of Austrian student found; headless skeleton found at foot of cliff.' Here's the last entry . . . '1961 . . . body of Utah prospector found—' "

"What's a prospector?" Jack interrupted.

"Someone who's looking for gold or silver," Simon answered. "A miner."

Henry continued, " 'Body of Utah prospector found, cause of death: gunshot wound to back. . . .' " He scanned the page, then turned it. "That's the end of the list. The rest of this is just stuff about the historical society."

"Okay," Simon decided. "We'll go see Sara Delgado tomorrow. Then we'll figure out what to do."

That night, right after the boys went to bed and Mr. and Mrs. Barker had disappeared into the family room to watch television, Henry snuck into the kitchen and took the phone out of its cradle. He sat on the cold floor, whispering 555–3233 to himself. Carefully, he dialed the number.

"Hello?" A woman answered.

Henry sat up straighter. "Um, is Delilah there?"

"I'm sorry, I can't hear you. Who are you trying to reach?"

Henry cleared his throat and glanced down the hall

in the direction of the family room, where the television droned. He said a little louder, "Is Delilah there?"

"Delilah? I think she might be asleep. Who's calling?"

"Henry. Henry Barker."

"Oh, the boy with the cat! Hold on, let me see if she's awake."

A minute later, Henry heard Delilah's voice. "Henry? Wait," she said quietly. And then, louder, "I'm just going to take the phone in my room, Mom."

He heard rustling on the other end of the line and then a door latching shut. Delilah's voice was breathless and eager. "I'm so glad you called! I have something to tell you. But first, did you look at the rest of the book? What did you find out?"

Henry took a deep breath. "In 1952, three boys from Texas disappeared on the mountain. Their bodies were never found."

"Hmmm," Delilah said. "Well, plenty of people have disappeared up there. At least it's not anything gross, like the heads chopped off."

Henry didn't know what to say. He knew Delilah was waiting for him to go on.

"What is it?" she asked impatiently.

"Well . . ." Henry paused. He peered into the darkened hallway again, making sure his parents hadn't heard him.

"What?" Delilah persisted.

Suddenly the phone call seemed like a mistake to Henry. What if she told her mother? They would all get in trouble then.

"You're not telling me something," Delilah complained. "After I helped you look through the newspapers and the books! After I went with you to Emmett's house! That's not fair."

"No, I am telling you," Henry said. "That's why I called."

"Then what is it? C'mon, just say it."

Henry took another breath. "We went up the mountain. Simon, Jack, and I did, a few days ago. Josie ran away, and we followed her, and we went up there, and Jack fell off a rock down into a canyon, and when Simon and I climbed down to get him, we found him on this ledge with three"— he gulped—"with three skulls."

The other end of the line was so quiet that Henry thought maybe she'd hung up. "Delilah?"

"Are you sure they were real? I mean, human?"

"Yeah, I'm sure," Henry said. "It was *unnerving*."

"Wow," Delilah said. She was quiet again. Finally, she said, "So you think they're the skulls of those three Texas boys? And they've been missing all this time?"

Henry nodded, then remembering the phone, said, "That's what we think. And now we can't figure out what to do. Simon thinks we have to call the police. But if we go back up the mountain with the police, and the skulls aren't there, it will be a *catastrophe*."

"Yeah," said Delilah. "And your parents will be really mad at you. I guess you can't know for sure the skulls are from those boys, right?"

"No," Henry agreed.

"But if they're not from those boys, they're from three other people."

"Right," Henry said. "So then we were thinking maybe we should go see that Sara Delgado girl, the one Emmett told us about, who lives near the cemetery. And try to figure out what happened to her on the mountain."

"Why?" Delilah asked. "How will that help?"

"Well, depending on what she says, we can decide if it's safe to go back up there." Henry thought it sounded like a stretch even as he explained it.

"I don't know," Delilah said. "She sounds pretty messed up."

"Yeah." Henry felt bleak.

"But okay," Delilah said quickly. "That doesn't mean we shouldn't do it. I want to talk to her."

"Me too."

"So then we should go to the cemetery and see what she has to say."

"Yeah," Henry agreed. "Hey—you said you had something to tell me. What was it?"

"Oh, right, I do." Delilah took a breath. "It's nothing compared to yours, but I was reading that library book I brought home, the one on Arizona legends, and it has some true stories too—or at least, the true stories the legends are based on. And one of them is about this guy, Adolph Ruth."

Henry had clamped the phone so close to his ear, it felt hot. "That name . . ."

"It was in the historical society booklet, I'm pretty sure. One of the first disappearances on the mountain."

"What happened to him?" Henry tried to remember.

"Oh, the usual. He was missing for six months, then his skull was found with two bullet holes in it," Delilah recited calmly. "But here's the interesting part: he was a treasure hunter, and he was looking for the Lost Dutchman's Mine."

"Did he find it?" Henry asked eagerly.

"Nobody knows for sure. But a year after Adolph Ruth's skull was found, they discovered more human remains with a lot of his belongings, including his checkbook. And there was a note inside, which said he'd discovered the mine! At the bottom, it had the words 'veni, vidi, vici.'"

Henry listened blankly. How could there still be so

many words he didn't know? "Is that a foreign language? What does it mean?"

On the other end of the line, he could hear the door unlatch and an impatient, "Delilah! Are you still on the phone? It's past your bedtime."

Delilah's faint apology followed. "Okay, I'll say good-bye."

"Now, please." The door clicked shut.

"I have to go," Delilah said reluctantly.

"But what does it mean?"

"It's Latin for 'I came, I saw, I conquered.' But listen to this: everybody at the time thought it meant he'd discovered the gold."

"Wow!" Henry exclaimed. "Adolph Ruth. We have to find out more about him."

"We have to find out more about a lot of people, including the three Texas boys," Delilah countered. She must have shifted position on the bed, because he could hear her mattress springs squeaking. "I really do have to hang up," she said. "But, Henry . . . what was it like?"

"What?"

"The mountain. What was it like up there?"

"Oh . . ." Henry hesitated. How could he describe it? "It was—well, it was really spooky, actually," he said slowly. "Quiet, with lots of trees and a weird feeling. Almost like someone else was up there. Watching us."

"That does sound spooky," Delilah said. "Maybe Superstition Mountain really is haunted. You think?"

"I don't know," Henry said. "That's what we'll ask Sara Delgado."

CHAPTER 17
AT THE CEMETERY

THE NEXT MORNING, the boys rushed through breakfast, not even bothering to squabble over the plastic toy at the bottom of the Cheerios box. They knew where the cemetery was: on the other side of the neighborhood, surrounded by desert, an easy bike ride away. The bigger challenge was getting out the door without interference from Mrs. Barker.

"What's up?" their mother asked suspiciously. "Why the big hurry?"

"No reason," Simon said.

As they scrambled to put on their shoes, she continued to watch them. "Have you made your beds?"

"Yes," they chorused.

"Fed Josie?"

"I did," Henry answered.

"Straightened your rooms? Because if I go back there and find clothes on the floor—"

"Mom! Can we go, please?" Henry begged.

"Go where?"

"Just for a bike ride, Mom," Simon told her impatiently.

"Again?" Mrs. Barker stood over them with her hands on her hips.

"We'll check in this time," Simon promised.

"We're going with Delilah," Henry volunteered. "She doesn't have anyone to play with otherwise."

A cheap appeal to Mrs. Barker's sympathies often worked rather well. "Okay," she relented. "It must be hard for her, not having any brothers or sisters. I think it's nice that you boys are trying to include her in your activities. Remember to put on sunscreen."

Jack opened his mouth to complain, but Henry grabbed his arm and pulled him up from the floor, where he was struggling with his shoelaces. "We'll take it with us," he told their mother, snatching a tube from the kitchen counter. "Come on," urged Jack, "she's waiting for us."

"Boys, listen to me! I want you to come home for lunch," Mrs. Barker called as they dashed out the door.

They rode to Delilah's house and turned into the driveway.

"You get her, Henry," Simon ordered, and Henry dropped his bike and ran to the front door. Moments after he knocked, a woman with wavy reddish hair and Delilah's same smile opened it.

"Hi," Henry said, a little nervous. "I'm the one who called last night."

"Oh, hi, hon," the woman said warmly, holding the door wide. "I'm glad to meet you. Delilah certainly has been talking about you Barker boys. You have such a pretty cat! We just love her. Come on in."

"Actually, we were wondering if Delilah—"

Delilah herself appeared before he could finish, slipping past her mother and joining Henry on the porch. "We're going to ride our bikes," she told her mother.

"Okay," her mother said easily. "You have your key? I have to go in to work later."

"Yeah, I have it," Delilah answered. She was already hoisting up the garage door to retrieve her bike.

"All right, have fun." Mrs. Dunworthy closed the front door, and Henry ran down the steps after Delilah.

"Your mom is cool," he said. "She doesn't ask a ton of questions about where you're going and when you'll be home."

Delilah nodded. "She doesn't bug me about that."

"And she doesn't even make you have a sitter when she's gone?" Henry asked enviously.

Delilah paused, looking a little embarrassed. "No, not anymore. That's too expensive. But I'm really responsible." She added this matter-of-factly, not like she was boasting. "And she trusts me."

"You're lucky," Simon said. "Our mom grills us about everything."

"But your mom's nice too," Delilah said. "She makes lemonade."

Henry wondered whether the kind of mom who made lemonade was also more likely to grill you about everything. He wasn't sure why that would be true, but it seemed like it might be.

Superstition Cemetery stretched over a large plot of land surrounded on three sides by a white concrete wall. The front of the cemetery had an ornate wrought-iron fence and a tall gate through which you could see rows of pale tombstones facing the street. It was so quiet and orderly, it almost looked like a classroom, Henry thought . . . except with graves instead of desks. Small, colorful bouquets of flowers leaned against some of the tombstones.

"Hold your breath!" Jack whispered as they walked toward the gate. They always held their breath when they passed the cemetery in the car or on their bikes—Henry couldn't remember why, exactly; something to do with not breathing in the spirits of the dead. But that clearly wouldn't work today.

"Jack, that's dumb," Simon said, rolling his eyes. "If you hold your breath the whole time we're here, you'll die."

"Don't call me dumb!" Jack lunged at Simon.

"Are they always like this?" Delilah said to Henry. She stepped between them. "You only have to do that if you're *passing* a cemetery," she told Jack. "Not if you're in one."

"Really?" Jack asked, doubtful.

"Really," Delilah replied.

"Look, the caretaker's house is over there." Simon pointed to a beige ranch with green shutters. The front door was flanked by two flower beds, and a teenage girl was kneeling next to one pulling weeds.

"Hey," Simon said, as they walked toward her.

She jumped to her feet, looking startled, and her dark hair fell forward, almost hiding her face. "I'm sorry for your loss," she mumbled quickly, backing away from them.

Simon and Henry looked at each other. "What loss?" Simon asked.

"Time heals all wounds," the girl replied, starting toward the door of the house.

"Wait," Delilah said. "Are you Sara Delgado? We want to talk to you."

"Sara, yes, yes, Sara. They're in a better place."

Jack tugged Henry's sleeve. "What is she talking about?" he asked. "I don't understand what she's saying."

"Me neither," Henry whispered.

"Nobody understands," Sara said. "Nobody can ever understand."

Simon walked slowly toward her. "We wanted to talk to you about the mountain. About what happened when you got lost up there."

Sara's eyes widened. Abruptly, she clapped both hands to her ears, backing toward the door of the house. "No, no, no, no, no. Not the mountain."

"Why not?" Delilah asked gently.

Sara stared at them. "Nothing will ever be the same," she said. She opened the door of the house and darted inside, slamming it behind her.

"Well, that helped a lot," Simon said unhappily.

"She's crazy!" Jack said.

"Shhh, Jack, not so loud," Henry warned. "She'll hear you." He turned to Simon and Delilah. "Why was she saying all that weird stuff? It didn't make sense."

"It sounded like what you say to people at a funeral," Delilah said. "You know, 'Sorry for your loss,' that kind of stuff."

Henry had no idea what people said to one another at funerals. He looked at Delilah curiously. "Really? That's what they say?"

"Yeah," Delilah answered.

"We didn't find out anything." Simon kicked the dirt. "We might as well go home."

"Hey!" Jack shouted. "Look! There's Josie!" He pointed toward the cemetery, and there, beyond the tall black gates, was Josie, trotting purposefully among the tombstones.

"Now, what do you think she's doing?" Simon asked. "She doesn't usually come all the way over here, does she?"

The truth was, none of them knew much about where Josie went during the day or how she spent her time when she wasn't in the house.

"Maybe she's chasing a gopher or something," Henry suggested. But she wasn't in her stalking pose—crawling low across the ground, then leaping.

"Let's get her," Delilah said.

Henry found this suggestion remarkably optimistic. It showed how little Delilah really knew Josie. But he followed as she walked through the gates, calling, "Josie! Josie, where are you?"

The cemetery was quiet. The morning sun glinted off the granite headstones. Henry decided it didn't feel scary, especially not compared to Superstition Mountain. It just felt peaceful and a little stern, like church. They wandered through the long rows, being careful not to step on the ground in front of the markers. "That's where the dead bodies are," Jack reminded everyone at regular intervals. Sometimes they came upon a white gravel path and walked on it for a while. Josie was nowhere to be seen.

"Where did she go?" Delilah asked.

"She's probably hiding," Jack explained. "She likes to do that."

Simon slowed down. "Wow," he said. "Some of these graves are really old."

Henry noticed they'd come to a part of the cemetery where the stones were crooked and chipped, discolored with age. The names and dates were difficult to read.

"This guy died in 1878," Simon said. "And his wife even earlier, 1872."

Delilah stopped before a small brown headstone that tilted to one side, with tufts of grass growing at its base. "Hey," she said.

Henry walked over to where she was standing. "What?" he asked.

He looked down at the stone, with its faded engraving. He could see the dates 1825 to 1896, but it was hard to read the name in block letters across the top.

"Julia something?" he asked Delilah.

"Julia Elena Thomas," she said slowly.

Simon walked over. "Julia Thomas? You mean . . ."

"Yeah. It's the name of that woman at the library."

"What?" Jack ran over. "What does it say?"

"It's nothing," Simon said, but his brows were crinkled. "Just the tombstone of someone with the same name as that librarian lady."

"The one with the black hair?"

"Yeah. But Thomas, that's a common name. And Julia too."

"Maybe it's just a coincidence," Henry said. But he wasn't so sure. He felt strange. Then a black blur caught his eye. "Look," he exclaimed in relief, "there's Josie!"

Josie was sitting on top of a headstone, her eyes wide, tail twitching lazily in the sun.

"Josie," Henry called to her, running between the rows of graves. Then he stopped in his tracks.

Below one of Josie's dangling paws, he could read the name etched on the tombstone in large, faded letters: BARKER.

CHAPTER 18

NAMES FROM THE PAST

SIMON, DELILAH, AND JACK nearly collided with Henry. Delilah gasped.

"Hey," Jack said, staring at the letters, "that's *our* name."

Simon crossed quickly to the headstone, scooped up Josie, and held her firmly against his chest. "You guys have to stop freaking out. Barker is a common name too! Come on. It doesn't mean anything."

But now Henry was turning, staring in every direction at the hodgepodge of century-old gravestones. "But look . . . Myers—that was the policeman's name, remember? And Waltz—that was the name of the guy with the gold mine, right?" His palms were damp, and he could feel the galloping beat of his heart. What *was* this place?

Simon ignored him, marching toward the cemetery gate. "Come on, let's go. It would make sense for that guy to be buried here. This is where he lived. If those other families have lived in town a long time, of course their relatives would be buried here. Like Uncle Hank—his tombstone is probably here somewhere too. Is that going to creep you out? You're making a big deal out of nothing, Henry."

Privately, Henry thought it would very much creep him out to see Uncle Hank's tombstone. It occurred to him that the inscription would say "Henry," not "Hank," and somehow seeing both a "Barker" and a "Henry" on tombstones in one day seemed too much to handle.

"I don't think it's nothing," Delilah said slowly, gazing at the tombstones. "People who are supposed to be dead are alive. Or people who are supposed to be alive are dead."

"Yeah!" Jack cried. "It's like they're GHOSTS."

"No, it's not. It's what Henry said, just a coincidence," Simon called impatiently.

He was almost to the gate, with Josie squirming in frustration, one paw batting his shoulder.

Henry shot a last nervous glance at the tombstone where Josie had been lying; at their own name chiseled across the front. He swallowed, wiping his damp hands on his shorts and scanning the rows of headstones. What if Uncle Hank were buried here somewhere? That seemed likely, and deeply unsettling. "Come on," he said to Delilah and Jack.

"Me first!" Jack cried. He pushed between Henry and Delilah, darting down the row after Simon.

"It IS weird," Delilah said to Henry, twisting one

braid. "Maybe it doesn't mean anything that the names are the same, but it's still strange."

"At least there wasn't a Dunworthy," Henry said. "It's freaky to see your own name on a tombstone."

Delilah flinched. "Yeah," she said, turning away from Henry. "It is."

Simon and Jack were already on their bikes outside the cemetery gates. Simon was struggling to keep hold of Josie, whose ears had flattened against her head in profound irritation.

"Are you going to ride with her like that?" Delilah asked.

"I'm going to try," Simon said, clamping her more tightly under his arm.

Delilah wheeled her bike close to his and stroked Josie's squirming body. "Shhh, Josie, we're going to take you home," she crooned. At least she wasn't calling her Princess, Henry thought.

"What should we do now?" he asked.

Simon stared at him. "Go back up the mountain and get the skulls," he said, as if the answer were obvious.

Henry stared at him. "But we didn't find out what happened to Sara Delgado."

Simon snorted. "We'll never find that out. She's not

going to tell us, and even if she did, we probably wouldn't be able to understand her. Look, it's still early, we have plenty of time to get up the mountain and back before dark."

"We're going *now*?"

"Don't you want to?"

Henry didn't know what to say.

Simon looked determined. "You were right, Hen. We shouldn't have left the skulls up there. They belonged to real people, maybe even to kids around our age. Nobody knows what happened to them but us."

"But I thought you said the skulls might not even belong to those Texas boys," Henry protested.

"Yeah, I did," Simon said slowly. "But still . . . no matter who they belonged to, we're the only ones who can get them and bring them back."

Henry shook his head. Simon was supposed to be the responsible one. "But Mom said we had to be home by lunch! We can't do this to her two days in a row."

It was a well-known fact in the Barker household that timing was everything. The thing you could get away with on an easy summer afternoon when Mrs. Barker was laughing on the phone with her sister was certainly not something you could get away with right before houseguests were expected, or when she was feeling pressured to meet a deadline, or when, for instance, you had just tested her patience with some questionable flouting of family rules the day before.

Henry knew, in his heart of hearts, if he were truly worthy of Uncle Hank's name, he should be eager for the adventure, but . . . he wasn't sure he wanted to go back up the mountain. He fidgeted miserably. Simon had seemed scared before, too. Why was he being so bossy?

Jack looked from one to the other. "This is boring! What are we doing?"

Simon considered. "Maybe Henry's right," he said reluctantly. "It might be better to do it a different day. But tomorrow's Saturday. We'll never be able to go then, or Sunday. Mom and Dad will be hanging around all weekend getting in our hair. We'll have to wait until Monday."

"MONDAY!" Jack groaned. "That's too long!"

"No, it's better that way, Jack," Henry told him. "They'll be less suspicious."

Simon's face brightened. "And know what else? If Uncle Hank went up into the mountains with poker players chasing after him as often as Emmett said, I bet he had a good map of the trails. I wonder if we could find it."

"A map! Maybe in the boxes in the basement," Jack said. "Let's go!"

He started pedaling vigorously down the road.

"Jack, wait," Delilah called after him, as they all began to follow. "You can't cross the street without one of us."

"A good map would really help," Henry said to her as he rode past. He wouldn't worry so much about climbing the mountain again if they had a map to guide them. He thought of the map in *Treasure Island*. With a good map, he would be ready for any adventure. Then he would be just like Uncle Hank: a true explorer.

When they clattered into the house, Mrs. Barker emerged from her study in surprise. "Are you back already? That was quick! I won't have to worry about you today." She smiled at Delilah, who was cradling Josie against her chest. "Hello, Delilah! Josie must have been happy to see you."

"Oh, she was," Delilah replied, just as Josie launched herself into the air and took off in a streak of disgruntlement.

"Mom," Simon began, "we were wondering if Uncle Hank had any maps."

Mrs. Barker raised her eyebrows. "Maps? Of what?"

"Oh, you know, this area," Simon continued casually.

"We're trying to learn our way around. Then it won't take us so long to get home when we're out bike riding."

Mrs. Barker appeared to accept this explanation. "Well, we certainly have maps of Superstition and the other towns in this area. Your father stopped at triple A in Phoenix and got a bunch when we moved here."

Simon shook his head. "That's not what I meant. We wanted Uncle Hank's maps," he said.

"Yeah," Henry elaborated. "We thought it would be cool to see the maps he used. Especially if there were old ones, you know?"

Mrs. Barker regarded them skeptically. "I don't see how an old map would be of any use to you. It probably wouldn't even have all the streets marked on it."

"Can't we just look through his stuff?" Simon pleaded. "It's all just sitting in boxes in the basement." He paused for emphasis. "It's such a waste."

That was clever, Henry had to admit. Mrs. Barker hated the idea of anything going to waste.

Their mother shrugged. "Oh, all right, I guess so. But I really don't think you'll find anything. Uncle Hank lived here for so long, I doubt he needed a map of the area. And I don't remember seeing one when I packed up his things." She pursed her lips. "Maybe try the desk, in the drawer with his coin collection. I left all those things alone."

"Uncle Hank had a coin collection? That's great!" Simon pumped a fist in the air. "Is it worth a lot of money?"

"I have no idea, sweetheart. It looked like mostly foreign coins to me, and there weren't many. Your father thought you three could divide it up."

"Divide it up?" Simon was instantly indignant. "Why can't I have the whole thing? I'm the oldest."

"It'll be worth less if you divide it up," Delilah said thoughtfully.

Henry scowled at both of them. "Hey! I'm the one who's *named* after him. If anyone should get it, I should."

"That's not FAIR!" Jack cried. "Is it, Mom?"

"This is exactly why your father thought you should divide it up." Mrs. Barker held the door of the basement open for them, flipping the light switch. "Go ahead and take a look in the desk, but I don't recall seeing a map."

They tromped down the basement stairs with Simon leading the way. It was annoying to Henry that Simon assumed he would get the coin collection. The hard thing about being in the middle, Henry often thought, was that you had none of the privileges of the oldest kid—the later bedtime, the bigger allowance, the chance to do everything interesting *first*—and none of the advantages of the youngest, with people generally humoring you, looking after you, and letting you have your way. What good came from being in the middle? It was impossible to get special treatment of any sort . . . apparently, not even the coin collection of the uncle you were named for.

Uncle Hank's desk was an old brown rolltop, with a grid of cubbies across the front and three big drawers on either side. Their mother appeared to have consolidated all their uncle's things into two of the drawers. There were the usual trays of pencils, pens, and paper clips; a stapler; a yellowed roll of Scotch Tape; a tangled knot of rubber bands; and then some more interesting items . . . a small, heavy snow globe of the Grand Canyon; a string-tied stack of old postcards, letters, and greeting cards; and a creamy sheaf of heavy paper with the name Henry Cormody printed in black script across the top. Not Hank, *Henry*. Henry traced the name with one finger.

"Too bad the stationery doesn't just say his first name, or you could use it," Simon observed, shuffling through the contents of the drawer. He sighed. "No map."

"Should we look in the boxes?" Henry asked. They

all turned to the towering row of cardboard boxes shoved into one corner of the basement. There were so many of them, sealed with packing tape. Their mother had labeled them in black marker by room—"Kitchen," "Living Room"—but there wasn't much more detail than that.

"That will take us forev—" Delilah began morosely.

"Hey, look!" Simon interrupted. "I bet this is the coin collection." He gingerly lifted a long metal box from the bottom of the second drawer and plunked it on the top of the desk. It was a dark rust color, with an interesting design etched over the surface. It looked old to Henry; it was dented and nicked, and the paint was peeling off in places, revealing gray metal underneath.

Delilah tapped the top of it. "I don't think that's a coin collection. My dad had a coin collection, and he kept the coins in plastic sheets, in a big binder . . . each one in its own little pouch."

Simon shook the box. Whatever was inside clinked and jangled noisily. "It sure sounds like coins," he said. He snapped open the metal lid, and they all peered inside.

Their mother was right. There weren't many coins—no more than a dozen, scattered across the surprisingly shallow trough of the box—and they looked nothing like regular American money. They were different sizes, discolored with age, and not exactly round—slightly misshapen, as if they'd been formed by hand.

"Wow," Henry said, picking up one of the larger ones. "These are cool."

He flattened it in his palm and squinted at the worn, dark surface. It had a man's profile on one side and a strange, florid design on the other, with scrolls and columns.

Simon dumped the rest of the coins onto the desk. He, Jack, and Delilah each took one.

"What does it say on them?" Jack asked.

"I don't know," Simon said. "It's something in a foreign language."

Henry tried to read the faint letters that marked the perimeter, encircling the design. "*H-I-S-P-A-N,*" he read. "*E-T . . . I-N-D.*"

"What's that?" Jack wanted to know.

Henry had no idea. He turned to Simon. "Maybe we can find out on the computer," Simon said, a bit skeptically.

The boys' computer use was severely limited because there was only one in the house and their mother and father kept all their work files on it, which made them chronically fretful that one of the boys would accidentally erase something when they were "fooling around." Also, Mrs. Barker thought they should play outside, not be stuck in front of a screen all day. And even in the short time they'd lived here, the internet in Superstition had proved so unreliable that there was hardly any point.

Simon had started to scoop up the coins to return them to the box, when Delilah grabbed his hand.

"Wait," she said. "What's that?"

Amidst the coins that Simon had poured onto the desk was a small piece of white paper, folded in half, about the size of the strip inside a Chinese fortune cookie.

Delilah pinched it open. She gasped. She looked at Henry and held it toward him.

CHAPTER 19

BOOKS, BONES, COINS

"VENI, VIDI, VICI," Delilah read.

Henry sucked in his breath and stared at her. The very same words! What did it mean?

"What is it?" Simon asked, taking the paper from Delilah.

Henry realized that neither he nor Delilah had told Simon and Jack about Adolph Ruth and the gold. "Do you remember me reading to you about Adolph Ruth?" he asked impatiently. "He was on the list in the historical society booklet, one of the first disappearances on the mountain. His skull was found with bullet holes in it?"

Simon's brow furrowed. "I remember the name. I remember thinking it was like Hitler, and how many Adolphs do you run into?"

"Well," Henry continued, "it took years for searchers

to find his remains, but they also found his wallet, and inside—"

"Inside was a note that had '*veni, vidi, vici*' written at the bottom," Delilah finished. "Which means 'I came, I saw, I conquered.' It's Latin."

"So?" Simon looked puzzled.

"Yeah, so?" Jack echoed. "Why's that important?"

"Because in the note, Adolph Ruth said that he'd found a . . . mine." Henry hesitated, looking at Delilah. "At the time, people thought he'd found the lost gold— that '*veni, vidi, vici*' meant he'd discovered the Lost Dutchman's gold mine."

"Really?" Jack cried, leaning on the top of the desk so hard it tipped forward, then thumped down with a jolt. "Do you think this little bitty paper means Uncle Hank found GOLD?"

"I don't know." Henry stared at the tiny slip of paper in Simon's hand. Had his uncle really written those words?

"Well, it could just be a coincidence," Simon said, but Henry could tell he was thinking the same thing Henry was: the day had been too full of coincidences.

Simon put the piece of paper back in the box, followed by all the coins except one, which he slid into his

pocket. Then he glanced up the basement stairs, lowering his voice. "All right, this is what we're going to do. I'll get Mom to let me use the computer and figure out what kind of coin this is. Henry, you're the fastest reader, you check the library book for stuff about those three Texas boys and about the other disappearances on the mountain. See if there's any pattern. Delilah, we'll have to leave from your house on Monday. Will either of your parents be there?"

Delilah shook her head. "It's just my mom, and she has to work."

"Good," Simon said. "But we're going to need an excuse to spend the whole day at your house."

Delilah thought for a minute. "We're digging a vegetable garden in the back. My mom would love it if you guys helped with that."

Simon smacked her shoulder appreciatively. "That's a great idea! That could easily take the whole day."

"But I don't want to dig a garden," Jack whined. "I want to go up the mountain!"

"We won't really dig the garden," Simon told him in exasperation. "We'll just *say* that's what we're doing, so we can be gone all day without Mom bugging us."

"Well, we'll have to dig some of it," Delilah said.

"Yeah," Henry agreed. "Otherwise, it'll be *obvious* we were doing something else." He felt doubtful about the whole scheme. What if Mrs. Barker asked if Delilah's mom was going to be home? They couldn't lie to her! It was okay to mislead her once in a while, but they didn't usually out-and-out lie. And she was very unlikely to let them go to Delilah's if she knew there was no grown-up around.

"Everybody has a job but me," Jack said anxiously. "What should I do?"

"Nothing!" Simon said. "Just try not to get in trouble for the weekend. Can you do that?"

Jack's lower lip quivered. He plopped down on the carpet and glared at his sneakers.

"Jack—" Simon began, and Henry was about to intervene, but Delilah got there first.

She knelt next to Jack. "I know what you can do. You can make a list of things for us to take up the mountain. Kind of like a survival kit. And then we'll fill up a backpack at my house on Monday."

Jack brightened, then said glumly, "But I can't write all that."

"You can draw pictures," Delilah suggested.

"Okay," Jack agreed. "I can do that!" He reached in the open drawer and took one of the pieces of paper that had *Henry Cormody* emblazoned across the top.

"Good," Simon announced, snapping the lid of the metal box and putting it back in the desk drawer. "Let's get to work." He bounded up the basement stairs with Henry, Delilah, and Jack close on his heels.

Henry spent the afternoon with the volume of Arizona history from the library open across his lap, thumbing through the thin pages. There was only a short chapter on Superstition Mountain, and it was mostly focused on warfare between the Spanish and the Indians. The

Spanish had explored the mountain looking for gold up until the mid-1850s. There was a rumor about a gold mine, discovered by the Spaniard Miguel Peralta, and a purported battle with the Apaches that was called the Peralta Massacre because it left so many Spanish dead. But the book said both the gold mine and the battle were "unconfirmed," and had become "one of the many legends about Superstition Mountain and its colorful, mysterious past." According to the book, the disappearances began in the late 1800s, and with the exception of Adolph Ruth and a few prospectors, they were again considered "unconfirmed." The three Texas boys weren't mentioned at all.

Henry thought back to the blindingly white skulls perched on the ledge of rock. It seemed so long ago that they'd found them. He scooted the heavy book off his lap and wandered into his mother's study. She was at her drawing table, leaning over a large sheet of paper, deftly shading a small disk of bone.

"What's that?" he asked.

"A kneecap. Patella," she added, her pencil making soft scratching noises across the page. "Don't they have beautiful names? This is the fibula, and here's the tibia." Her pencil traced the contours of two long bones on one side of the paper.

"Mom?"

She didn't look up. "What is it, Hen?"

"You've drawn skulls, right?"

"Of course. Those can be hard."

"Why?"

"Because you have to get the proportions exactly right. We all have an instinctive sense of what a human face should look like, you know? Even when it's just bones, not a face, everybody has a sense of where the eyes, nose, and mouth should be . . . how they should fit in relation to each other. With other bones, people don't have a clue."

Henry slumped on the floor, watching her hand on the page. He took a breath and asked carefully, feigning indifference, "Have you ever drawn a skull that had a dent in it?"

"Sure," his mother said. "That's a common kind of skull fracture. It's called a Ping-Pong fracture."

"Really? Why is it called that?"

Mrs. Barker stopped drawing, her hand hovering over the page. "Hmmm . . . I don't know. Maybe because those fractures are usually the size of a Ping-Pong ball? Or maybe it's because the surface of the skull caves in the way a Ping-Pong ball does when it gets dented. I bet that's it."

"How do you get a Ping-Pong fracture?" Henry asked.

Mrs. Barker turned back to the paper and started sketching again. "Any number of ways. Bumping into something sharp. Falling and hitting your head. Getting banged on the head with something."

Henry nodded slowly. He pictured the skull on the cliff, with its shallow indentation. What had happened to that boy? Had he fallen and bumped his head? Or did somebody hit him on the head and kill him?

He stood up suddenly.

"What, nothing more about skulls?" Mrs. Barker asked.

"Nope," Henry said. One good thing about his mother—she found bones so interesting herself that it would never have occurred to her to wonder why he was asking so many questions.

"All right, I'm finished for the day," his mother said, leaning back in her chair just as Simon and Jack appeared in the doorway.

"Hey, Mom, if you're done, could we use the computer?" Simon asked.

"Till dinner? Please?" Jack added.

Mrs. Barker wavered. "What for?"

"We're trying to figure out what kind of coins are in Uncle Hank's collection," Simon replied. That sounded so legitimate, Henry realized, because it happened to be true.

"Well, I guess," Mrs. Barker conceded. "But just until dinner, and no messing around with any of my files, or your father's, okay?" As she left the room, she added, "I don't know how much luck you'll have—the internet was down earlier today."

"Thanks," Simon said. He tugged the coin out of his pocket and held it up to Henry and Jack. "Come on," he whispered. "Let's find out where this is from."

They all crowded around their mother's computer, and Simon navigated quickly to the internet.

"How can you look it up if you don't know where it's from?" Jack demanded. It was a fair enough question, Henry thought—like looking up a word in the dictionary to figure out how to spell it, which teachers were always telling you to do, ignoring the fact that if you didn't already know how to spell it, it was very difficult to look it up.

"Watch," Simon said. "I'll Google the words on this side." Squinting at the tarnished surface of the coin, he typed "hispan et ind" and "coin" into the search area and hit the return key.

The computer ground and whirred for several seconds, then a long list of matches appeared. Near the top were "Spanish Silver Milled Coinage" and "Spanish Dollar."

"Wow, you found it!" Henry cried. "It's from Spain!"

Simon shrugged modestly.

"Now let's see if we can find this exact coin. I can't see the date on it, can you?" He handed the coin to Henry. Henry took it over to the lamp on Mrs. Barker's drawing table and scrutinized it beneath the white blaze of light.

"One . . . eight . . . something . . . four." He turned excitedly to his brothers. "It's really old! At least a hundred fifty years, don't you think? Maybe more."

"Ooooh, is it worth a lot of money?" Jack asked. "Is it real silver?"

"It's definitely real silver. That's what they used back then," Simon said. "Hey, here are pictures. Is it one of these?"

Henry carried the coin back to the computer and held it in the glow of the screen, next to a column of photos showing silver coins on black backgrounds. The coins were similar, with the profile of a severe-looking man on one side and an elaborate design on the reverse, a shield with a crown over it, flanked on either side by columns. Henry scanned the photos. The coins in the picture were crisper and cleaner; the one in his hand was so faded and dark.

"Wait," he said, pressing his index finger against the screen. "What about that one? It's the same, isn't it?"

Simon took the coin and held it next to the image, comparing them, then flipped it over. "Good job—that's it." He bumped fists with Henry.

"Who's the lady with the ponytail?" Jack wanted to know.

"It's not a lady, it's a man," Simon told him. "Back in the old days, the men had long hair like that."

"Like Henry used to have," Jack said, turning to Henry and adding helpfully, "when everybody thought you were a girl."

Henry frowned. "Nobody would have thought these guys were girls." They looked too brave and noble, long hair or not.

"Nope," Simon agreed. "They were kings." He peered

at the screen more closely. "And anyway, I don't think it's a ponytail. It looks like a ribbon. Listen, this is what it says on the coin in English." He pointed to the caption below the picture of the coin and read, " 'Ferdinand the Seventh, by the Grace of God.' That's on the front, and 'King of Spain and the Indies' on the back. That must be what '*Hispan et Ind*' stands for: Spain and the Indies."

A Spanish king! Henry squinted at the man's profile.

"Does it say how much it's worth?" Jack asked, bouncing impatiently.

"Let's see." Simon typed "Spanish dollar what's it worth" in the search area and tapped the return key. He scanned the results and then said, "That's weird. Even though it's so old, it's not worth much money. Here's one from 1802, probably older than ours, in much better condition, and its only value is forty bucks." Simon sighed in disappointment. "That coin collection is nothing special."

Henry bristled. "Yes, it is! It belonged to Uncle Hank. That makes it special. And the coins are still really old, from a whole other country. Anyway," he added, "they might tell us something about the mountain."

"Yeah," Jack cried, leaning against Simon's shoulder

to get closer to the screen. "And forty dollars is A LOT! Where does it say that?"

Simon squirmed free. "Jack—"

"Boys!" Their mother's voice drifted down the hallway. "Would one of you please set the table for dinner?"

"It's Jack's turn," Simon answered.

Henry expected Jack to protest, but he merely seemed annoyed. "Don't look at stuff without me," he warned.

Simon obligingly closed the windows on the computer and slipped the coin back into his pocket. "I wonder how Uncle Hank got a Spanish coin."

"Maybe he found it on the mountain," Henry said thoughtfully. Skulls, coins, treasure . . . what else was up there? He wondered.

CHAPTER 20
NECESSITIES AND SUPPLIES

THEY SPENT THE WEEKEND lying low, as Simon called it. They played darts in the basement; they helped their dad weed the walk; they found an old rope from a tire swing and strung it between two trees about a foot off the ground so they could play tightrope walkers, and then snake pit, and then river of piranhas. It was just like any other weekend. Part of Henry felt relieved. It was nice to be normal for a while, doing normal things, not finding skeletons or talking to crazy people or stumbling through graveyards that had a tombstone with your own last name on it. Every time he thought about the mountain—about going up the mountain again, back to the canyon—a chill crept through him.

But the other part of Henry knew this was the test. Could he live up to Uncle Hank's name or not? Was he brave enough to go up the mountain and bring back the skulls? He wanted to believe he was that brave inside, and the only reason nobody knew it was there hadn't been a chance to prove it yet . . . sort of the way the old lamp in the book *Aladdin and the Magic Lamp* lay around for centuries with a genie inside, but nobody knew it because they hadn't happened to pick it up and dust it off. Was it possible that Henry could have lived his whole life without a chance to discover his inner fearlessness? He wanted to think so, but secretly had his doubts.

On Sunday afternoon, he was contemplating this and other not-so-happy thoughts while his father sat at the kitchen table paying bills.

"Is Uncle Hank buried at the cemetery?" Henry asked Mr. Barker.

"Why, no, Hen. He was cremated. Why do you ask?"

"I just wondered," Henry said, and then quickly, making it a more general inquiry, "Do you want to be cremated?"

As it turned out, Mr. Barker had a surprising amount to say on this subject. No, he did not want to be cremated. He found the "blazing inferno" too unnerving, though of course he would be unable to feel anything, being dead. Nor did he want to be buried, as a matter of fact, because he was claustrophobic and he didn't like the idea of being underground covered by dirt. Mrs. Barker walked into the kitchen at this point and added, "Though of course you won't know that or feel that, being dead." Nor did Mr. Barker want to have his body donated to science—Mrs. Barker's preference—because he didn't want medical students standing around making fun of him.

"Honey, that's ridiculous," Mrs. Barker interjected. "They would never do that. You're being paranoid."

"No, I'm not. They DO do that. You're forgetting that I had a friend who went to medical school—Carl Lisi—and he told me all about it." He turned to Henry. "Now, what I'm really paranoid about is that your mother will decide to donate my body to science even though I don't want her to. Do you hear that, Henry? Happy to have them transplant any useful organs, but I don't want my body left at the mercy of a bunch of incompetent grad students."

Mrs. Barker rolled her eyes. "Go ahead. Tell Henry what you want instead."

Mr. Barker tilted back in his chair and stretched his arms expansively. "Well, this is what I have in mind: a nice mausoleum."

Mausoleum. Henry liked the long, musical sound of the word. "What's that?" he asked.

"It's an above-ground tomb," his father explained, "made out of stone. That's fitting, right, Henry? Like a crypt, no windows, but big enough for the coffin to sit inside."

"Now tell Henry how much that would cost," Mrs. Barker said.

"Pshaw, what does the cost matter?" Mr. Barker winked at Henry. "I'm sure you'll spare no expense for me when I'm gone. You'll want to do it up right."

Mrs. Barker groaned. "It would cost a fortune. And what a waste!"

"Oh, well, too bad," Mr. Barker said philosophically. "It's my dying wish. You're my witness, Henry."

"Don't pay any attention to him," Mrs. Barker told Henry. "He's kidding around."

Mr. Barker pulled Henry close, and whispered, "Just don't let her donate my body to science! I'm begging you."

"I can hear that," Mrs. Barker called over her shoulder as she left the room. "And it won't be up to the boys, you know. . . ."

Mr. Barker raised his hands helplessly. "Rats! Foiled again."

Henry crossed his arms on the table and rested his head on them, thinking about the mountain. "A mausoleum does sound nice," he said, and then, "Dad, are you scared of dying?"

"Yes," his father answered promptly. "But your mother isn't."

"Why not?" Henry asked.

"Oh, you'll have to ask her. Maybe because it's natural. And because there's always something left—we return to bones. And you know how she likes bones."

Henry nodded. He stared at the glittering ring of droplets around the base of his father's glass of iced tea.

"What's the matter, sport?" his father asked. "You seem gloomy."

"Nothing," Henry said. "Just thinking."

To Henry's mounting dismay, the plan to spend the day at Delilah's on Monday went off without a hitch.

"That is so nice of you boys, to help with their garden!" Mrs. Barker said. "It's a very neighborly thing to do. And I get the impression that Delilah's father isn't around much, don't you? So I bet they really appreciate it. Just make sure you dig exactly where Mrs. Dunworthy tells you to, okay?"

"We will, Mom," Simon assured her while Henry looked guiltily at his shoes. He hated lying to their mother, but what other choice did they have? She would never agree to their plan. It was the only way to bring the skulls back where they could be identified. Henry squared his shoulders. It was the right thing to do, even if their mother didn't know it yet.

Mrs. Barker continued, "And call to let me know how it's going. Maybe I could come over to see the garden this afternoon. I'd like to meet Delilah's mother. I feel bad that I haven't introduced myself before now."

"Oh, I don't think we'll finish it today," Simon said. "You should come tomorrow when it's all done."

"Okay," Mrs. Barker agreed. "And it's all right for you to stay there for lunch?"

"Delilah said it was fine," Henry said carefully. That was technically true; Delilah had said it was fine with her mother for them to be there all day. Not that they were actually going to be there.

The boys were starting to leave when Jack cried, "I forgot my paper!" At first Henry didn't realize what he meant, but then he remembered it was the list of supplies for their trip up the mountain. Jack dashed back to his

bedroom and reappeared, waving it triumphantly in one hand.

"What's that?" Mrs. Barker asked, reaching for it.

Henry froze. "Oh, it's nothing—" Simon started to say, but their mother took the paper from Jack and studied it.

Nobody moved, and Jack's eyes widened in horror.

"Jack, these are good drawings!" Mrs. Barker said, beaming at him. "And on Uncle Hank's stationery too. It looks so official. So many little pictures—what's this?"

Jack gulped. "Candy."

"And this?"

"More candy."

Mr. Barker, hurrying through the kitchen on his way to work, tousled Jack's hair and laughed.

"And what about this?"

"Soda," Jack explained.

"It's like a menu. Or a grocery list," their mother observed cheerfully, handing the paper back to Jack. "Okay, boys, good luck with the garden!"

As they hurried outside, she held the door for them and waved innocently from the stoop. Josie, by contrast, darted between her legs and under the bushes, watching them from the shadows with her skeptical golden eyes.

Henry felt a leaden mix of guilt and resolve as they rode away. He could hear Simon scolding Jack as they rounded the corner of Delilah's street.

"You have to be careful! What if she'd figured out what it was? It's a good thing you can't draw."

"I can too draw!" Jack cried. "She said it was GOOD! And Mom's an ARTIST."

"Well, she couldn't tell what anything was."

Henry rode between them. "Do you really think we should be doing this?"

"Doing what?" Simon asked.

Henry swallowed. "Going up the mountain again."

"Aw, come on, Henry! Don't chicken out."

"Yeah," Jack said. "Why are you so scared?"

Henry's jaw clenched. "I'm not! It's just . . . I have a bad feeling about it."

Simon turned to him in frustration. "What? We've been up there before. Nothing happened. We know where we're going this time, and we'll bring plenty of water."

Henry looked at Simon in disbelief. "What do you mean, 'nothing happened'? Jack fell down the side of a cliff, we found three skulls, and a tree almost crushed me! And it was really creepy! Don't you remember what it felt like up there? You're supposed to be the responsible one," he finished plaintively.

Simon steered into Delilah's driveway and stopped, turning to face Henry. "I'm tired of being the responsible one! It's boring to follow the rules all the time. Come on, Uncle Hank must have gone up the mountain dozens of times. And he lived into his eighties. We'll be okay. Don't you want to? It's an adventure!"

Henry propped his bike by the garage, staring miserably at the asphalt driveway. What Simon said was true. Uncle Hank had gone up and down the mountain lots of times; Emmett Trask said so. And he wasn't afraid.

"Don't be a scaredy cat, Henry!" Jack said loudly, so loudly Henry was afraid that even inside the house, Delilah could hear. He stiffened. He wanted to tell Jack that expression didn't make any sense. There was nothing scared about Josie. She was the reason they'd all gone up the mountain in the first place. But he only frowned. "You're not the boss of all of us, Simon," he said.

"I know that," Simon snapped. But suddenly he relented. He draped his arm over Henry's shoulder. "It's okay, Hen," he said. "Tell you what: if it's gets weird up there, and you feel scared, we'll come right back. I promise. We won't even get the skulls."

"Hey—" Jack protested.

"Really?" Henry asked.

"Really," Simon said.

Delilah was waiting at the front door. "What's taking you guys so long?" she asked.

"Nothing," Henry said. "We're coming."

"Here's the list!" Jack clamored, thrusting it into her hands. "Can you tell what it says?"

"Sure," Delilah answered dubiously. "That's something to drink, right?"

"Yep! Soda."

"And that's . . . grapes?"

"Candy!"

"What's this one?"

"Band-Aids."

"That's smart, Jack," Delilah said. "We should take Band-Aids, just in case."

"See?" Jack turned to Simon smugly.

"Well, that *was* smart," Simon admitted. "Smarter than showing Mom the list, at least."

Jack stuck out his tongue, but Delilah pulled them into the house before it could go any further.

"Do you have a compass?" Simon asked her. "A compass would be good."

Delilah nodded. "Yeah, in the box of camping stuff in the basement. I'll go look for it. You guys can start filling up the backpack. It's on the kitchen counter."

Simon headed immediately through the archway to the kitchen, but Henry and Jack stood in the foyer, looking around. Other people's houses were so interesting, Henry thought—like a giant version of the inside of someone's backpack. There were so many different ways that their owners' personalities could shine through—in furniture, knickknacks, how messy or neat a place was. Delilah's house was tidy but stuffed full, every table and shelf packed tight with things. In the living room, there were dozens of framed photographs. They covered the walls and crowded every square inch of the end tables.

"Wow, there are so many pictures," Jack said.

Henry walked around looking at them. A much smaller Delilah with fat cheeks grinned toothlessly from a baby swing; Delilah clung to the railing at the top of a slide; Delilah leaned forward on the shoulders of a man with a big smile and crinkly brown eyes. Her father, Henry decided.

"Here it is!" Delilah cried jubilantly, bursting through the basement door. She had a scratched silver compass in one palm. "I can't believe I found it. What else do we need?"

"Supplies!" Simon called from the kitchen. "Is it okay to take anything on the counter?"

"Yeah, I put all of that out for us," Delilah said, glancing at Jack and adding, "but leave room for Jack's list."

Henry and Jack followed her into the kitchen, where Simon was stuffing bottled water into Delilah's backpack, which was a disconcerting neon shade of pink.

"Hey," Jack complained, "that's not soda."

"It's better than soda if we get thirsty," Simon said. "The soda has a lot of salt in it."

Henry nodded. Sometimes it just seemed that Simon knew everything about everything. "Water is a *necessity*," he told Jack morosely.

Using Jack's list, Delilah raided the Dunworthy kitchen for a modestly healthy assortment of snacks that included granola bars, potato chips, and peppermints.

"Don't you have any other candy?" Jack asked, outraged.

"No," Delilah said apologetically. "My mom says it's bad for your teeth."

Since candy appeared to make up more than half of the items on Jack's list, the packing process was conveniently abbreviated. Jack looked at what was left. "What about the Band-Aids?" he grumbled.

"Oops, in the bathroom," Delilah said, heading down the hall. She reappeared with a fistful in wrappers.

"Okay," Simon said, zipping the backpack shut. "That's everything. Let's go. We'll take turns carrying this— Jack, you first."

"No way!" Jack recoiled. "That's a girl's backpack."

"I'll carry it," Delilah said, yanking both straps over her shoulders. It was bulging, and Henry could tell the water made it heavy.

"Fine, but you're going to have to carry it too, Jack," Simon said, "or you can't come with us."

Jack made a face.

"What about our bikes?" Henry asked.

"I'll write my mom a note that we're going for a ride," Delilah said. "We can leave them at the end of the street by that vacant lot and cut straight across the hills to the mountain. It'll be faster."

"Great," Simon said. "And I'll call our mom and check in, like we promised." He dialed from the wall phone, and Henry listened desperately for his mother's side of the conversation, but all he could hear was Simon's.

"Hey, Mom, it's us, we're at Delilah's. Yeah, we're about to get started, but then we'll be outside so we won't hear the phone. . . . No, it's fine, Delilah's mom doesn't care." Henry tensed. What if Mrs. Barker asked to speak to her? But the conversation continued smoothly. "Yeah, we will. Definitely by dinner. Okay, Mom, bye!"

He clicked the phone back in place and turned to them gleefully. "That was easy. She just wants us home by dinner. And it's only eleven! We have tons of time."

"What about the vegetable garden?" Henry asked. "We have to dig some of it."

"We can do it when we get back," Simon said dismissively. "Come on, let's go."

Henry felt sick to his stomach. He thought of Uncle Hank, going into the mountains all by himself, with angry, gun-toting poker players hot on his trail. It was no use. He and his great-uncle were nothing alike.

Delilah scrawled a quick note to her mother and locked up while the boys climbed on their bikes. As they pedaled down the driveway, away from the safe little house and the quiet, safe neighborhood, Henry saw Josie strolling across a lawn. She stood at the edge of the sidewalk watching them, only the tip of her tail twitching. Far ahead, Superstition Mountain's dark bluffs hovered over the desert, waiting for them.

CHAPTER 21

BACK UP THE MOUNTAIN

THEY HID THEIR BIKES behind a scraggly clump of sagebrush at the end of the street and hurried toward the mountain. They had to cross the foothills first, and Jack, who ran ahead in a fit of enthusiasm, was soon dragging his feet and demanding water.

"You can't have it yet," Simon told him. "We need it for the mountain, when we're really thirsty."

"I'm really thirsty now," Jack complained.

"That's because you're running," Simon said. "Just stick with us, and you won't get tired."

"I'm not thirsty because I'm running, I'm thirsty because I'm HOT!" Jack argued.

"Come on, Jack," Henry said. "See? That's the path. And look, our sticks are still there."

The twigs they had painstakingly used to mark their

way days ago still seemed to be in place, propped at odd angles in the dirt, some of them falling over . . . but visible.

"That'll help," Simon said happily. "I didn't know how we were going to find the big boulder otherwise."

Henry glanced at him suspiciously. "I thought you said we knew our way now."

"Well, we do. But that didn't mean it would be easy."

They began climbing the twisty, pebbly path up the mountain, past the low-growing shrubs and bright patches of wildflowers, into the occasional loose grove of oaks. Henry's heart began to pound in his chest, its *beat-beat-beat* matching his feet's quick pace. He could sense the change in the air, its strange, oppressive pulse. Even Jack stopped talking, as if the place required silence. Despite the heat, Delilah shivered, looking around with quick, worried glances.

"See what I mean?" Henry asked her.

"Yeah," she whispered. "It is spooky."

They kept climbing. The path forked again and again, and the markers were harder to spot.

"Is that one?" Henry asked.

"I don't know," Simon said in frustration. "It could be, or it could just be a stick that fell and got stuck in the ground. I can't tell."

Sometimes trees leaned close to the path, speckling their backs with shade, but mostly there were no trees, just the hard, tawny rock, patches of spiky grass or brush, and the sun bearing down.

"Now can I have a drink?" Jack whined. "I'm so thirsty."

"Okay, okay," Simon relented. He set the backpack on the dusty ground and unzipped it, unscrewing the cap on a bottle of water.

Jack gulped it greedily, dousing the front of his shirt.

"Save some for us, Jack," Henry said. He scanned the slopes in every direction. "Are we close to the rock where Jack fell? There are more bushes and trees here, and it seems like we've been walking long enough."

"Yeah, it does," Simon agreed. "I hope we haven't passed it."

"We haven't passed it," Jack said confidently. "I remember what it looked like."

How could he? Henry wondered. No part of the mountain looked familiar. The trees, the rocks, the messy scrub of brush along the path looked like everywhere and nowhere. Nothing was distinct. He took a swig from the bottle. The cool water made him feel better. At least they had plenty of water, and it was still early in the day. Surely everything would be all right.

"Look!" Simon said. "There's the needle. We're getting close."

Up ahead, over the ridge, they could see Weaver's Needle, its craggy pinnacle rising forlornly amid the jumble of smaller peaks.

"That's a weird-looking rock," Delilah said.

"The old miners and pioneers used it to figure out where they were on the mountain," Simon told her.

"That's handy," Delilah said. "So where are we on the mountain?"

Simon hesitated. "Somewhere west of Weaver's Needle."

They kept walking. Henry carried the backpack for a while, until the straps bit into his shoulders. Then Delilah took it.

"My legs hurt," Jack said. "Why is it taking us so LONG?"

"Because the path is getting steeper," Henry told him. "It's *arduous*."

"Hard-yu-us?" Jack asked. "Like, hard for you and us?"

"Arduous," Henry repeated, shaking his head. "But that's kind of what it means."

"Hey," Simon said. He stopped in the middle of the path. "Delilah, give me the compass."

Delilah fished it out of the bottom of the backpack and handed it to him. "What's the matter? Do you think we're going in the wrong direction?"

"Not exactly," Simon said. "But there were so many forks."

Jack plopped onto the ground and dropped his head in his hands. "Then we'll never find the rock!"

"No, listen," Simon persisted. "It's a CANYON. You can't miss a whole canyon. I think we should go this way, through the trees. We'll come to it eventually."

Henry swallowed. The trees hung over them, and the strange, heavy air pressed like a stone against his chest. "I don't know, Simon. I don't think we should go off the path."

Delilah nodded. "We might get lost."

"We can mark the way, like we did before," Simon said firmly. "Plus, if we can just find the canyon, we can figure out the way home from there."

"Okay," Jack said. "Let's go!" He crashed through the twiggy bushes and started off into the trees.

"Wait!" Henry cried. "What if we can't find it? What if we end up on a different part of the mountain and can't find our way back?" He thought of Sara Delgado, with her glazed, blank face.

Simon clapped his hand to his forehead in frustration. "Okay, Henry, what do you want to do? We've been climbing for almost two hours. It will take us nearly that long to get home. Do you want to have to come up here again? With Mom and Dad watching our every move? It was hard enough this time."

Henry held back. He looked at Delilah.

She took the compass from Simon and cupped it in her palm. The silver disk glinted in the sun. "We have this," she said to Henry, closing her fingers lightly over it. "It's my dad's compass. It's good luck. If we get lost, we should at least be able to figure out which direction is home."

"Come on!" Jack cried. Henry could see his blue shirt waving like a flag through the clumps of vegetation.

"Listen," Simon said, zipping the backpack and settling it over his shoulder. "It's two o'clock. Let's walk east for an hour. If we haven't found the canyon, no matter where we are, we'll turn around and use the compass

to go down the mountain. Okay, Henry? We'll definitely be back before dinner."

It made sense, but Henry still felt a prickle of foreboding on the back of his neck. "Okay," he agreed, as Delilah and Simon hurried after Jack into the woods.

CHAPTER 22
ALONG THE EDGE

THEY PICKED THEIR WAY through brambles, then wended between the straight, rough trunks of trees. Henry could hear furtive sounds all around them . . . the fluttering of birds overhead, dry rustlings in the undergrowth.

"Do you think this is where the mountain lions are?" Jack asked, slowing down.

"No," Simon said. "They like rocks. Remember those pictures in our animal books? They're always on ledges or cliffs. Not where the trees are."

"And they're shy, anyway," Delilah added calmly.

"They are?"

"Yep. They're scared of people."

Henry said nothing. He was thinking that any mountain lion pictured on a cliff had probably gone through woods to get there, and why would a mountain lion be scared of people when it could eat people? But it wouldn't be helpful to point this out when Jack seemed reassured.

"Hey," Delilah said. The others stopped and turned toward her. "There are fewer trees this way. I can see the sky."

To their right, the grove had thinned, and there were patches of bright blue shining through the branches.

"I bet that's the canyon," Simon said eagerly. "Come on, you guys!"

They ran, their feet pounding against the ground, with Simon leading the way, the backpack flopping against his shoulder, and Delilah holding the compass outstretched. Abruptly, the ground pitched beneath them, sloping and opening up.

Henry gasped. They were at the edge of a deep gorge. Steep reddish brown slopes plummeted sharply to the pebbly floor, with patches of trees and shrubs growing haphazardly along it.

"Is it the same one?" Henry asked uncertainly. It was hard to tell. The ravine was narrow and twisty, like the first canyon, but where was the ledge with the skulls?

"I think so," Simon said. He scanned the gorge. "Over there! Isn't that where Jack fell? The side we climbed?"

"Maybe." Henry shielded his eyes from the fierce sun. "But I don't see the rock with the skulls on it."

"I think it's just hard to see from here. We'll have to climb along the top to get closer."

Delilah's eyes widened. "Climb sideways? Along the edge? It's so steep! We'll fall."

"No, we won't," Simon said.

Jack jumped in. "Are you scared?"

Delilah glared at him. "No. And I'm not the one who's going to fall, either."

Henry studied the jagged wall of the canyon. He felt the strange sense of dread circling. "What about climbing down to the bottom and then back up to the ledge where the skulls are?"

"It'll take too long," Simon said. "We wasted too much time finding the canyon."

"We could keep walking here in the woods," Delilah suggested. "That'd be safer."

"We could try that," Simon said doubtfully, "but I think we'll end up heading away from the canyon. It would be faster to climb across the wall here, till we can see the skulls."

Jack bounced on his toes impatiently. "Let's go!"

Delilah turned the compass in her hand, stroking her

thumb over it. "It's getting late. I guess we don't have a choice."

"You go first, Henry," Simon decided. "Then Delilah next, then Jack. I'll hold on to the backpack and be last."

"Okay," Henry said reluctantly.

He began to inch along the wall of the canyon, stepping sideways, feeling for grooves and footholds with his sneakers. He kept his eyes glued to the top of the cliff. He glanced down once, but the bottom of the gorge was so far below it made him dizzy. When his sneakers slipped against the side, loose stones sprayed into the air, tumbling through space until they disappeared. It was all too easy for Henry to imagine what would happen if he lost his grip.

"Are you guys there?" he called over his shoulder. He didn't want to risk turning around.

"Yeah," Delilah answered, not far behind him.

"We're here!" Simon yelled. "Try to go a little faster, okay?"

"I'll try," Henry mumbled. He reached out his hand and felt for a purchase, crouching against the rough rock. The sun burned his back. Sweat trickled behind his ears and dripped inside his shirt. Far below, a large bird wheeled over the crooked chute of the canyon. It looked like a vulture.

"Hey!" Simon called. "I think that's the ledge."

"Yeah!" Jack shouted. "I remember!"

Henry glanced up, following the direction of Simon's finger. Some distance ahead, just beneath them, he could see a rocky shelf jutting over the ravine.

"I don't see the skulls," he said.

"You can't from here," Simon answered. "We're too far above it. We should start climbing down."

Henry grumbled to himself. Climb across, climb down . . . Simon acted like it was as easy as steering a bike! He began to lower his body against the wall of the canyon, dangling one foot and tapping tentatively for anything that felt sturdy enough to step on. He shook damp strands of hair out of his eyes.

"What time is it?" Jack asked.

"Hang on, I'll check," Delilah began, then cried sharply, "Oh! The compass!"

In an instant Henry turned to see the silver compass hurtling through the air, with Delilah grasping frantically after it.

It bounced against the side of the canyon and started to roll. Delilah leaned way out, taking another swipe at it.

Henry reached for her. "Delilah, don't—"

"It's my dad's!" she cried. She lost her hold and began to slide, clutching futilely at the canyon wall. Stones rained through the air all around her.

"Hold on!" Simon yelled to her. But it was too late. They watched in horror as she bumped and tumbled down the side of the canyon, desperately clawing at rock.

CHAPTER 23
INTO THE CANYON

"Ahhhhhhhh!"

Delilah's piercing scream was followed by a faint, sickening thud when her body finally struck the canyon floor, some sixty feet below.

"Delilah! Delilah, are you okay?" Henry cried.

He could see the pale square of her T-shirt far beneath them.

"Delilah?" Simon echoed. "Can you hear us? Are you hurt?"

They strained into the silence, but no sound came back to them.

"Do you think she hit her head?" Jack asked. "Maybe she's knocked out."

Henry turned anxiously to Simon. "What are we

going to do? What if she's really hurt? DELILAH!" he yelled again.

This time, they heard a moan, and Henry saw the T-shirt move.

"Ohhhh!" Delilah cried, her voice catching in a sob. "My leg!"

"Can you stand on it?" Simon called.

"Owww! No! It hurts! It hurts!"

"Hang on," Simon told her. "Don't move."

He looked at Henry, his face pale beneath the spiky crown of his hair. "We need to get help."

"But we can't leave her here," Henry protested.

Delilah squirmed on the ground below. "Where's my compass?" she wailed.

"Forget the compass," Simon said. "It doesn't matter."

"No, I need it! You have to find it. Henry? Please."

"Okay, okay," Henry answered. He peered at the slope below. He could see the dusty smear where Delilah had lost her grip and begun to slide. "I'll find it." He tried to sound more confident than he felt.

"Listen, Henry," Simon said. "I'll climb down and stay with her. You take Jack and go for help. Can you find your way back?"

Henry swallowed. "I think so. I don't know."

"What about the skulls?" Jack asked. He scrambled closer to Henry, nimbly gripping the rocks.

"We can't do anything about them now," Simon said.

Jack groaned. "See? I told you it was a bad idea to let her come. She's ruined everything!"

"Shhh," Simon said. "She'll hear you. It doesn't matter now. We have to get help."

Henry shook his head slowly. "You're the one who should go," he said to Simon. "You know the way better than I do."

Simon looked at him, hard. "But that means you'll have to stay here with Delilah. On the mountain."

"I know," Henry said. His lungs felt so tight in his chest he could barely breathe.

"Henry . . ."

"Just go," Henry said. He squared his shoulders. "I'll climb down and stay with her until you get back."

"Henry," Simon said again, "I don't know that we can make it back here before dark. We'll go as fast as we can, but—"

"It's okay," Henry told him. "Just hurry." He scanned the slope below him. Where was the compass? He longed for the shiny clarity of its arrow, pointing steadily in a known direction. He looked down the funnel of the gorge to where Delilah lay on the canyon floor.

Simon thought for a minute, then nodded grimly. "Okay, maybe you're right. Here, you take the backpack. You need it more than we do." He took out a bottle of water, then zipped the backpack and carefully looped it over Henry's outstretched arm. When he took his hand away, Henry felt a pang of hopelessness, as if he were losing his last defense against the mountain's strange magic.

"Don't worry, Henry," Simon said. "We'll come back as fast as we can. Jack, let's go."

Henry slid the backpack over his shoulder and watched as his brothers scrambled along the cliff above him, with Simon calling instructions and Jack reaching for foot- and handholds, crawling and hopping from one to the next.

"Hurry," Henry said, mostly to himself.

But Simon heard him. "We will," he answered.

"What's going on?" Delilah called. Henry could barely make out her pale upturned face. "Did you find the compass?"

"No, but it's probably right below me. I'll look for it on my way down."

"Your way down? You're coming down here?" Delilah sounded shocked.

"Yes," Henry said, making his voice firm and loud to compensate for the quaking in his stomach. "Simon and Jack are going for help."

"Why doesn't Simon stay here with me?"

Henry scowled. Of course Delilah thought Simon would be the better one to stay. Truth be told, he *was* the better one to stay. He wouldn't be scared. He would know what to do in an emergency. And he knew the kind of science-y stuff that could be helpful when you were out in the middle of nowhere, with rocks and trees and wild animals all around.

"Because Simon will be able to get help faster," Henry told her, beginning to climb down the side of the gorge.

Delilah watched him skeptically. "I don't think this is such a good idea," she called. "We'll both end up stuck down here."

Henry didn't think she sounded sufficiently grateful. Or at all grateful. Also, she seemed to have an annoying excess of opinions about her pending rescue. "This never would have happened if you hadn't dropped the compass," he yelled back. "Would you rather be down there by yourself?"

Silence from the canyon, and then "No. . . . Hey, look for the compass!"

"I told you I would," Henry answered. He continued his descent into the canyon, feeling the watchful eyes of the mountain all around him.

CHAPTER 24
LOST AND FOUND

HENRY PICKED HIS WAY down the slope, avoiding the loose dirt where Delilah had slid. He stopped twice, to wipe sweat out of his eyes with his shirt and to take another sip of water. He didn't see the compass anywhere.

Delilah watched from below. Every once in a while, she called out, "Watch that root," or "Go to the right—it's not as steep." More often, she asked, "Did you find the compass?"

Henry could see her clearly now, propped against a boulder. Her clothes were covered in dust, and her left leg lay stiffly in front of her.

Finally, the pitch of the ground changed, flattening. Henry half stood and scrambled the rest of the way to the bottom of the gorge.

He brushed off his pants and ran over to Delilah. "Does it still hurt?" he asked, leaning over her.

She cringed and nodded. Her leg was red and swollen, the knee scraped and dark with blood.

"Hey, you're bleeding," Henry said, awed.

"I know!" Delilah said, wincing. "Good thing we have Band-Aids."

Henry unzipped the backpack and dug around in the bottom until his fingertips brushed the paper wrappers of the Band-Aids. He handed her two and watched somberly while she opened them and tried to orient them on her knee to cover the blood.

Finally she gave up. "It's too big a cut," she said dejectedly, wadding the Band-Aids into a sticky ball. "And you know what else? I can't stand up. I already tried. My leg is killing me. And"—she covered her face with her hands—"I lost the compass." Henry was suddenly afraid she might cry.

"It's okay," he said quickly. "You can get another compass."

"It's my dad's."

"I know, you keep saying that. Is that why you're so upset? Do you think he'll be mad at you?" Henry reached into the backpack again and took out the granola bars.

He wasn't really hungry, but it was something to do, and it might make Delilah feel better. He handed her one.

Delilah tore open the foil and took a bite. "He can't get mad at me. . . ." She stopped. "He died."

Henry stared at her.

"It was a long time ago," she said quickly. "When I was six."

"Oh." Henry didn't know what to say. He'd never met anybody who didn't have a father. He thought of all the photographs in Delilah's living room, the man with the crinkly brown eyes. "What did he die of?" he asked finally.

"A car accident," Delilah said.

"Oh," Henry said again.

She didn't say any more. But Henry immediately understood why she couldn't lose the compass and why she couldn't replace it with another one.

"I'll keep looking for it," he said. "Maybe it rolled all the way down to the bottom."

Delilah was quiet.

"Do you want some water?" He fished around in the jumble of wrappers and bottles.

"I guess." Delilah took the bottle without enthusiasm and drank a little. She shifted against the rock. Her face crunched with the effort.

Henry glanced around. The sun was high in the cloudless sky, blazing into every crevice of the ravine. The crooked, pebble-strewn path that must have been a creek wound through the canyon floor, flanked by a few squat trees, gray-green shrubs, and patches of yellow and blue wildflowers. The walls of the canyon seemed even steeper from down here, rising sharply on either side to the woods at the top. Henry saw no sign of Simon and Jack. Good: they must already be on the path down the mountain. Suddenly, he caught his breath.

"Look!" he said, touching Delilah's shoulder. "There are the skulls!"

On a ledge high above them, three white globes flashed in the sun, neatly lined up along the rock.

"Wow, that's pretty spooky," Delilah said, her eyes wide. "It's like they're watching us."

"Yeah . . . watching the whole canyon," Henry agreed. Like *sentinels*, he thought to himself.

"Why would someone have put them there?"

"I don't know. To scare people?"

"That's what I was thinking," Delilah said. "But why?"

Henry shrugged, feeling an urge to change the subject. "What time is it?"

"Almost three."

"There's plenty of time for Simon and Jack to get home and back here with help before it's dark."

"Yeah," Delilah said softly.

Henry wondered if she was thinking the same thing he was. What if Simon and Jack got lost? Then who knew how long it would take them to get down the mountain? And what if they couldn't find their way back? There were so many paths, and the mountain was full of canyons. But it didn't help to think that way. Henry shook his hair out of his eyes and stood up.

"I'm going to look for the compass."

"Okay," Delilah said. She squinted up at him, shielding her eyes with her hand. "Thanks, Henry."

Which made Henry feel bad for what he'd thought about her before, that she was bossy and ungrateful. He set off along the creek bed, his sneakers crunching against the loose stones. He heard a bird call, a sharp, echoing cry, and he looked up to see the dark shadow of something passing overhead—a hawk or another vulture, he wasn't sure. The canyon floor was a maze of boulders and rocky inlets. He kept scanning it for a flash of silver or glass, but he saw nothing. He was almost directly under the ledge with the skulls now.

"Henry?" Delilah's voice drifted to him. "Did you find the compass? I can't see you anymore."

"I'm here," Henry answered. "But I haven't found it yet." He sighed, ready to turn back.

Then something caught his eye. Amid the pebbles at his feet was something long and white, gleaming in the sun.

A bone.

Henry sucked in his breath. He crouched down, gently brushing the stones aside for a better look. Then he realized it wasn't just one bone. There were bones everywhere.

CHAPTER 25

REMAINS FROM LONG AGO

"DELILAH!" HENRY CRIED. "There are bones here, a bunch of them."

"What do you mean? Where?"

"Near where the creek used to be. Mixed in with the stones."

Henry sorted through the rocks, gently clearing a space around the bleached white bones. He remembered the list of dead people in *Missing on Superstition Mountain*; the bones found at the bottom of a canyon. Were these human? Did they belong with the skulls? He couldn't tell. He saw something larger, a long, white bone with a row of flat teeth protruding from it. It was a jawbone, he realized, way too long to belong to a person.

"I don't think these are human bones," he told Delilah, relieved. "Maybe a deer."

Then, as he scanned the area, Henry glimpsed something large and dark under a shrub a short distance from the creek bed. He walked over to it, thinking it was fur, the remains of some big, brown animal. But when he touched it tentatively with his finger, it felt hard. Like a shoe.

"I found something," he called to Delilah.

"What is it?"

"I don't know . . . something made of leather."

Carefully, Henry extricated it from the undergrowth—a hardened pair of leather pouches with a strap connecting them. They were so worn and tattered they were falling apart. The leather looked ancient to Henry, as if it had been washed with rainwater and dried by the sun a thousand times.

"It's a saddlebag," he said loudly. "And it looks really old. I bet the bones are from a horse."

"Let me see."

Carrying it gingerly with both hands, Henry walked back along the creek bed to where Delilah was lying. He knelt beside her and set the crumbling saddlebag on the ground.

"Wow," Delilah said. "Who do you think it belonged to?"

"I don't know. Somebody from a long time ago."

"Look at the fancy buckles."

Even though they were blackened with tarnish, Henry could see that the buckles on the saddlebag *were* fancy, intricately decorated with swirls.

"Let's see if there's anything inside," Delilah said. Gently, she unbuckled the flap of one of the pouches and held it open while Henry slid his hand into the darkness. His fingers closed around something small but surprisingly hefty. It was a little sack, also made of leather, tied with a strip of rawhide.

"What's in it?" Delilah asked, leaning forward, then moaning. "Ow!" She fell back against the rock, clutching her leg.

"Are you okay?"

"Yeah, it just hurts. I hope they come soon."

"Me too," Henry agreed. He gently untied the string and pried open the neck of the sack, brittle with age. Dust and bits of leather sifted into his lap. He squeezed two fingers through the opening and felt pieces of hard, cool metal.

"It's money," he told Delilah, pinching one of the coins and lifting it into the sunlight. It was silver, as tarnished as the buckle. Henry recognized it immediately. "Delilah," he said urgently. "Look! *Hispan et Ind*—they're Spanish coins, just like the ones in Uncle Hank's coin box." They were identical: the severe profile, the columns and shield.

"From the Spanish explorers!" Delilah cried. "They must have been left in this canyon a long time ago. They could have been here for two hundred years!"

"I wonder if they're from the Peralta Massacre," Henry said.

"Wow," Delilah said. "I remember that. I read about it in my book from the library—when the Apache Indians fought the Spanish, leaving the bones of men and mules all over the canyons." She reached across him. "Let me check the other bag," she said, lifting the flap.

"What's this?" Delilah's hand emerged holding a thick, tattered piece of brown paper, folded twice. She sat forward and opened it on her lap. "Oh! Henry, look! It's a map."

It was a crude map drawn in ink on dark heavy paper, the edges frayed and crumbling. At first, Henry couldn't tell what anything was. There was no writing on it.

"Are those roads?" he asked Delilah, pointing to a few thin lines.

She peered at them. "I don't think so. I think those are creeks—see how wavy they are?"

Henry looked more closely. "Then these must be peaks," he said, "for the mountain?" He traced the points that encircled the map, and then ran his finger along one of the channels through the middle of it. "What's this?"

"It must be a canyon," Delilah said. "Because look, there's a creek in the middle of it. And these are trees." She pointed to small, spiky lines all along the creek. "Hey . . ." She lifted the map gently into the air, and turned it. "I think this is our canyon, Henry, the one we're sitting in right now! Look at the way the creek bed zigzags . . . and this ledge on the map, it might be the ledge with the skulls."

"You think it's the same one?" Henry asked. "There are so many canyons here. How can we tell?" His gaze swept the uneven ground, the brown walls of rock that jutted in from either side. There were so many nooks and crannies, and the shrubs made it hard to see the contours of the gorge.

Delilah brushed stones and twigs aside to clear a small place on the ground, where she spread the map flat. "If we put it like this—look at the drawing—does it fit the way the creek bed turns?" she asked.

Henry nodded slowly. "But what's this on the side? It looks like another little canyon." Delilah squinted at the map, then scanned the wall of rock behind them, in the opposite direction from where Henry had searched for the compass. "If it is, it would be right over there, around those rocks. Go have a look, Henry. Maybe another canyon connects to this one."

Henry scrambled to his feet and ran the short distance to the outcropping of rock. It looked like the rest of the canyon wall, craggy and creviced, and he was about to turn away in disappointment when he realized that there, behind it, almost obscured by boulders, was a narrow channel.

"Hey!" he yelled to Delilah. "There's an opening."

He edged sideways between the sharp rocks, picking his way between the steep walls, thinking that at any moment the inlet would end in rock. But it didn't. A thin dirt path twisted along, and Henry felt a growing thrill of excitement. This must be how it was for Uncle Hank, he thought—during his days as a cavalry scout, when he set off for uncharted territory, exploring someplace nobody had been before. This was how it felt to discover something new. Henry realized he didn't feel scared at all. He felt eager, as if the mountain were nudging him along.

A minute later, the walls slanted away and the sky opened over his head. He found himself standing alone in a small, hidden canyon.

CHAPTER 26

"THE MOUNTAIN IS ALIVE..."

"HENRY? WHERE ARE YOU?" Delilah's voice sounded faint and far away.

"I'm coming back," he called. "It's a little secret canyon. You would never know it was here."

He ran quickly through the narrow passageway back into the ravine, where Delilah had apparently been dragging herself across the ground to follow him. She was panting and wincing in pain, still holding the map.

"What are you doing?" Henry protested. "You should have stayed where you were."

"I didn't know where you went," Delilah said. She glanced up at the sky. "It's going to be dark soon."

"Yeah," Henry said. He walked over to where she'd left their things. Gently he closed up the leather pouch of coins and tucked it in a side pocket of the backpack.

Then he picked up the backpack and saddlebag and carried them to where Delilah was lying.

"Do you want something else to eat? More water?" he asked. He helped her lean against a rock. Her leg looked even more swollen now. The skin was turning darker.

Delilah clutched her leg, breathing heavily. "I'm not hungry," she said. "Do you think they'll be back soon?"

Henry nodded. "I bet they're climbing up the mountain right now."

"Good. I hope so." She leaned her head against the rock and closed her eyes.

"Does it still hurt a lot?" Henry asked.

"Yeah."

"Do you think it's broken?"

"Probably."

Since she didn't seem to want to talk, he picked up a stick and began to poke the bushes. A rabbit sprang out from underneath one, making him jump. It darted off through the canyon, its white tail bobbing.

"What was that?" Delilah asked, opening her eyes.

"Just a rabbit," Henry said. "I scared it with my stick."

She stirred slightly. "So there's a whole other canyon over there? Hidden behind the rocks?"

"Yeah, a secret canyon. It's a lot smaller than this one."

"Then this old map is right."

Henry nodded. "I wonder who made it. I mean, were they soldiers, or explorers, or"—he hesitated—"maybe gold miners?"

"I know," Delilah said, "I thought that too! What if it's a map to a gold mine? But I was looking at it the whole time you were gone, and there's no special mark or anything . . . nothing that looks like gold."

Henry squatted on his heels, dragging his stick in the dirt, thinking about old maps and lost gold mines.

"Henry?" Delilah's voice was soft.

"Yeah?"

"Do you hear that noise?"

"What?" Henry turned back. Her face looked pale and anxious in the dusk.

"That rustling noise."

Henry listened for a minute, straining into the bluish quiet. He did hear something, a faint distant crackling, then silence.

"It's probably another rabbit," he said staunchly.

"It sounds bigger than a rabbit."

"Maybe it's a raccoon?" Henry tried to think of other animals that weren't scary.

"It feels weird here . . . like the mountain is alive," Delilah said haltingly.

"I know," Henry said. "It really does feel that way up here."

Delilah leaned forward a little, holding the map. "Can you put it away now? So nothing happens to it?"

Henry unzipped the side pocket of the backpack and was just placing the map inside when—*boom!*—there was a noise like a clap of thunder.

A piece of rock flew off the wall of the canyon several yards away from him, landing with a bang near his foot.

Delilah screamed.

Henry whirled around, looking in every direction, his heart thumping so hard in his chest he thought his rib cage would split open. He gazed at the cliffs on either side, at the seam of land where the woods ended and the canyon walls plummeted.

"What was that?" Delilah cried. "It sounded like a gun!"

"Shhh," Henry whispered. "I think it was."

How could that be? The canyon was dead silent again, but the air seemed to thrum with anticipation. Delilah was sitting up, leaning on one arm.

"Henry," Delilah said softly, her voice filled with dread. "Do you remember what it said in *Missing on*

Superstition Mountain? The list of people? Some of them were shot. What if somebody's *shooting* at us?"

Henry couldn't stop his legs from shaking. "Why would they do that?"

Delilah grabbed his arm. "Do you think they can see us? Do they know where we are?"

Henry met her panicked gaze. "I'm not sure." He looked around, desperately scanning the top of the ravine.

"What should we do?" Delilah asked, her breathing quick and urgent.

Henry tried to think. "We shouldn't stay in the open like this." Simon would say they were sitting ducks. He pushed the saddlebag under the bushes where the rabbit had been. Hurriedly, he covered it with rocks and dirt till no trace was visible. Then he crouched next to Delilah, sliding the strap of the backpack over his shoulder. "If I help you, can you stand?"

"I don't know," Delilah said. "It hurts so much."

"Listen," he whispered. "We'll go into the little canyon. Nobody will be able to see us there."

"I don't think I can move that far," Delilah said.

"Yes, you can," Henry told her. "I'll help you."

She took a deep breath. "Okay, I'll try."

Delilah struggled onto one knee and began to crawl, dragging her hurt leg behind her, moaning softly. Henry took her arm and carefully helped her to her feet. She pressed her fist to her mouth to keep from crying out. Awkwardly, leaning against each other, they stumbled through the brush to the boulders that hid the entrance to the other canyon. Delilah's face was covered in sweat. Henry knew it wasn't from the heat.

"Are you okay?" he asked, as she limped into the narrow passageway. "Is your leg worse?"

"It's worse when I move," Delilah said hopelessly.

They continued a short distance, then leaned against the walls, listening to the silence.

"Henry, what's going on? Why would someone be shooting at us?"

Henry swallowed. "I don't know. Maybe it was an accident. Maybe somebody was hunting, and they thought they saw a deer." He shook his head. "Maybe it wasn't even a gunshot."

Delilah looked at him doubtfully.

Now that the canyon was so quiet again, it was hard to imagine the shattering sound from before. Who could be up here shooting at them? It didn't make any sense.

After a minute, she said, "I keep thinking about that list of dead people. The skulls with bullet holes in them."

Henry nodded grimly.

"Say something," Delilah whispered.

Henry took a breath. "Do you think this is what happened to Sara Delgado? Is this why she went crazy?"

They looked at each other in the gathering gloom. Delilah covered her face with her hands. "It's almost dark! Where are Simon and Jack? What if they got lost?" She dropped her hands suddenly, stricken. "Or what if whoever's shooting at us has been shooting at them too?"

Henry stiffened. "No," he said, trying to make his voice steady, desperate to stop the tidal wave of fear. "They didn't get lost. Simon is smart. Simon always knows what to do. He'll come back, I promise."

"You promised you'd find my compass, too," Delilah said quietly.

There was nothing to say to that. Henry leaned back against the rock, watching the sky. It turned from gray to navy, the velvety color just before night.

And then it was dark. The canyon's rocky walls had become nothing more than vague, blurred shapes. The night was full of noises: twigs crackling, leaves whispering against each other.

"Do you hear that?" Delilah kept asking.

"Yeah," Henry would say.

"What do you think it is?"

"Just some animal, probably."

The air had turned cooler. They moved back toward the entrance to the passageway so they could see into the canyon and sat against the boulders, huddled close to each other for warmth. Henry thought of all the people who had climbed Superstition Mountain looking for gold . . . and how many had never been seen again.

"What's that?" Delilah hissed, grabbing his arm. She pointed into the darkness.

Henry gazed out, his eyes tracking the canyon floor. "What?"

Then he saw it: a dark shape moving low to the ground, skirting the bushes and trees.

CHAPTER 27

SOMETHING IN THE NIGHT

A CHILL RIPPLED through Henry. "It's too small to be a person," he whispered to Delilah.

They watched as the shape drew closer, darting and then stopping, shrouded by darkness.

"What could it be?" Delilah whispered.

"I don't know," Henry said, "but it's coming closer."

Suddenly the black shape streaked toward them, and Henry saw two glowing golden eyes.

Delilah gasped.

"Oh!" Henry cried. "It's JOSIE."

Josie trotted up to the boulder and wove between Henry's legs, her tail twitching.

"Josie!" Delilah cried, scooping her up and hugging her.

Josie purred tolerantly.

"How'd you get here?" Henry asked, collapsing against the rock in relief. Josie was no protection at all, he knew that. But she was also never, never afraid. He scratched the flat part of her head as she gazed calmly into the darkness.

Just then, distantly, Henry heard dogs barking. Dogs and voices, a faint but unmistakable scuffle of activity in the woods above the canyon.

"Henry!" It was his father's voice, echoing over the gorge.

"We're here!" Henry shouted, leaping to his feet. "Down here!"

Delilah's face split wide in a grin. "Josie must have followed them."

Or led them, Henry was thinking. Josie never followed anyone.

"Here!" Henry yelled again, waving his arms.

He could see the dim beams of flashlights on the cliff above and dark figures gathering there. Two dogs were straining and barking. Josie's ears flattened with disapproval.

"We see you, Henry!" his father called. "Is Delilah with you?"

"Yes, she's here," Henry answered.

"Delilah, honey? Are you okay?" A woman's voice, worried and breathless, drifted through the night.

"Yeah, Mom, I'm fine," Delilah called back. Henry could hear her voice break, and he thought she might be about to cry, but then she gripped the boulder and pulled herself upright.

From the edge of the cliff they heard "Oh, thank God! Hold on, honey, we're coming."

The rest of the night passed in a blur for Henry. After hours of eerie silence, the canyon erupted in a chaos of noise and activity. The search party consisted of Mr. Barker, Simon, Mrs. Dunworthy, Officer Myers, two other policemen, and two medics. Only the medics and the policemen climbed down into the canyon to retrieve Henry and Delilah. The others waited at the top, calling questions and encouragement. The two police dogs were tied to a tree, barking and lunging at the ends of their leads. Delilah tried to keep hold of Josie, but she turned stiff and furious and soon squirmed free, leaping into the night. Henry hated to see her go, but he felt oddly certain this time that she'd find her way home.

The medics brought a splint, a stretcher, and ropes. As they leaned over Delilah, checking her pulse and blood pressure, Officer Myers peppered Henry with questions—Why did they come up the mountain? How did they find the skulls? How long were they in the canyon? Did they see anything unusual?—and fixed him with a piercing stare each time he tried to answer. Simon had clearly told the police about the skulls, but Henry wasn't sure what else, so he tried to answer carefully. He told about the gunshot and showed Officer Myers the chipped rock where the bullet had ricocheted. But though the policemen arced their flashlight beams across the canyon floor, kicking at stones and bushes, they were unable to find the bullet. What Henry didn't mention, didn't even hint at, was anything about the other bones . . . or the saddlebag . . . or the map.

As the medics crouched on either side of Delilah and stabilized her leg, Officer Myers said, "So that's it? You two stayed in this area the whole time?"

"Yes," Delilah answered promptly, giving Henry a quick, stern glance. "Here, Henry, take my backpack." He understood that she was thinking the same thing he was: keep quiet about the rest of it.

"We were over here when we got shot at," Henry said, pointing obligingly. "But after that, we just hid by those big rocks." He gestured vaguely.

"And you didn't see anyone or anything?"

Henry shook his head. "Nothing *sinister*," he said.

"All right, then," Officer Myers said gruffly. "We'll file a report, but without the bullet, it's going to be hard to apprehend anyone."

Why does he seem so annoyed? Henry wondered. Probably because they'd come up the mountain, after his explicit warnings.

The medics managed to immobilize Delilah enough to carry her up the side of the canyon. The two other police officers climbed to the ledge to collect the three skulls, with Simon directing them from above. Officer Myers held on to Henry, alternately lifting and pulling him up the slope.

Henry glanced back into the gorge twice, at its steep, twisted contours, dark as a pit. He couldn't see the hidden canyon from here. What other surprises did the mountain hold? He gripped the strap of the backpack and thought of the map and the coins. As grateful as he was that he, Delilah, Simon, and Jack would soon be off the mountain, he knew in his heart they would all be coming back.

CHAPTER 28
HOME

AND THEN, SUDDENLY, everyone was together at the top of the cliff, in the dark chilly woods, ready to start for home. Mr. Barker greeted Henry with a bout of scolding and a bear-hug of relief. Simon grabbed his arm and whispered to him excitedly about the trek to get help. He and Jack lost their way twice and drank all the water, but they'd eventually found the path again and made it home. He'd promptly told Mr. and Mrs. Barker and the police about the skulls ("I had to, Hen! They kept asking why we went up the mountain, and we needed their help to bring the skulls back anyway."). In the end, he'd been allowed to lead the search party to Henry and Delilah because even his thorough description of the canyon and the location of the ledge hadn't been explicit enough to guide the police. Unfortunately, Jack, who'd begged repeatedly to be part of the rescue mission, had been required to stay home with Mrs. Barker. She insisted that she be left with at least one family member in the event that nobody returned.

Mrs. Dunworthy, wearing sneakers and flower-print pants and looking like she'd never hiked a mountain in her life, kept stroking Delilah's hair and fussing over her hurt leg. The medics transferred Delilah to a stretcher, and with the two police dogs whining and straining ahead, the group started down the rough trail. It was a slow trip—the path dark and rock-strewn, the flashlights barely adequate, the medics taking extra care with the stretcher—but after a while, the slope changed, and Henry could see the houses of Superstition, lit up along the highway like beads on a necklace.

The next morning, Henry slept later than he ever had in his life. When he opened his eyes, the sun was streaming through his bedroom window, and he could hear Jack talking loudly in the kitchen. He crawled out of bed and checked to make sure Delilah's backpack was still tucked securely in the corner of his closet, behind a jumble of baseball mitts, balls, and shoes. Then he hurried down the hall. With the drama and fuss of the return, and his mother and father firing questions, Henry had had no chance to tell Simon and Jack what he'd found.

They looked up eagerly when he walked into the kitchen. Jack raced around the table to hug him.

"I thought you were going to DIE!" he cried.

"Jack," Mrs. Barker scolded. "That's not nice. What would you like for breakfast, Henry? You slept so late! You must be starving."

"Did Josie come back?" Henry asked, glancing around at the bright, familiar kitchen.

His mother looked at him curiously. "Where did she go? She's been lying on the deck all morning."

"Oh, good." Henry sighed happily. He got a box of cereal from the cupboard and scraped his chair back from the table. Simon and Jack crowded next to him.

"Delilah has a broken leg!" Jack reported. "It's in a cast that looks like a boot! And she's on crutches."

"Is she in the hospital?" Henry asked.

His mother set a bowl, spoon, and glass on the place mat in front of him. "No, but she didn't get home until after midnight. I talked to her mother this morning. It was a clean break, no involvement of the growth plate, so it should heal quickly—three or four weeks. She'll be fine." She poured orange juice into Henry's glass. "Did you know she lost her father a few years ago?"

Henry nodded, and at his mother's surprised expression, added, "She only told me that yesterday."

"But I suppose you knew her mother works for an insurance company outside of Phoenix and is often gone during the day?"

Henry looked at Simon.

"And I doubt you made much progress on their vegetable garden yesterday, did you?"

The three boys stared resolutely at the table. Even Jack knew better than to open his trap at a time like this.

Mrs. Barker's mouth was a thin, mad line. "I can't believe you lied to me!"

"It wasn't a lie—" Simon started.

"Simon, don't even try. You deliberately deceived me, and you know it. You boys are going to stay *right here* for the rest of the week, maybe longer. Your father and I haven't decided yet. Do you understand?" She straightened her glasses on her nose and glared at them.

Simon nodded glumly. "Yeah, yeah. Sorry, Mom."

"You should be sorry," Mrs. Barker said.

"We are," they chorused, but she didn't seem particularly appeased.

"I have Delilah's backpack," Henry said. "I have to give it to her."

"Don't you worry about that," his mother replied. "I'll make sure she gets it."

"No, that's okay," Henry said quickly. "I want to take it to her myself, when she's better. She doesn't need it now anyway. School is *months* away." He felt cheered by that. They had the whole summer ahead of them.

"Did Dad call about the skulls yet?" Simon asked.

"Not yet," Mrs. Barker said. "I told you I would let you know as soon as he did."

"But they're testing them now, right?" Simon persisted. He turned to Henry. "The police took them to the coroner's office last night. They're comparing dental records and looking at that one skull with the dent in it. They said they might know something by this morning."

Mrs. Barker glanced at Henry. "One of the skulls had a Ping-Pong fracture, I understand."

He nodded sheepishly.

She came to stand behind him, running her fingers gently through his curls. "That's the only reason I'm not more upset with you boys. I know you were trying to do something good by bringing those bones back so they could be identified." She leaned over Henry, looking

directly into his eyes. "But the mountain is too dangerous a place for children! Or for anyone. Do you hear
me, Henry? Poor Delilah, with her broken leg! And you
gave her mother such a scare, you have no idea. She's lost
one family member already." She shook her head. "We're
lucky nothing worse happened to any of you."

As soon as Henry finished breakfast, the boys dressed
with speedy indifference and fled the house. They climbed
into the fort of the swing set, where Mrs. Barker couldn't
hear them.

"So what happened in the canyon?" Simon demanded.

"Were you scared?" Jack asked.

Henry took a deep breath and told them everything—
about exploring the creek bed, finding the saddlebag,
the Spanish coins, the map, the secret canyon.

"Is it a treasure map?" Jack shouted.

"Shhhh," Henry whispered. "Nobody knows but us."

"Where is it?" Simon asked. "Did you bring it back
with you?"

Henry nodded. "It's in Delilah's backpack. In my
closet."

"I want to see it!" Jack cried.

"I'll show it to you, but not while Mom's snooping
around."

Simon whistled under his breath. "Do you think it shows where the gold is?"

Jack scooted over to the slide and whizzed down it. "We have to go back and find it! We'll be RICH!"

"I don't know. Delilah spent a long time looking at it, but she didn't see anything that seemed like a symbol for gold or a mine. It might just be an exploring map." He paused. "Like Uncle Hank would have used. But the secret canyon was really cool! You have to walk through this tiny alley of rocks. You can't tell it's there at all."

Just then, the sliding door opened and their mother stepped onto the deck. "Boys? That was your father calling," she said soberly. "They've identified the skulls. Apparently, they belonged to three boys from Texas—teenagers—who disappeared on the mountain in the 1950s."

Simon and Henry exchanged glances. So it was the three boys after all! They had been missing for sixty years. And, Henry thought, nobody would ever have known what happened to them—the skulls might never have been found—without Jack falling off that boulder and rolling into the canyon.

"Can they tell how they died?" Simon asked.

"No, not yet. The coroner said that might not be

possible unless they can find the rest of the skeletons. It looks like one of them may have fallen and hit his head; that was the cause of the Ping-Pong fracture. But the bone had started to heal, which means the fall didn't kill him. He might have died days later. The police are going back to search the area this week."

Henry stiffened. If the police went into the ravine again, would they find the passageway into the secret canyon?

Their mother rested her hand on the deck railing, studying them. "You three are staying put today. I don't even want you riding your bikes on the street."

"Okay, okay, Mom. We get it," Simon said in exasperation.

"Good." She gave them another long, serious look, then went back into the house.

"That's bad," Henry said. "If the police go poking around up there, they could find the gold mine before we do!"

"If there even *is* a gold mine," Simon said. "We don't have proof of anything. It could just be a legend." He saw the look on Henry's face and amended, "Yeah, I know, we still don't want them looking around up there."

Henry let out a long breath. "What can we do? We're grounded."

"It's not fair," Jack complained. "We did all the work."

"Well," Simon said thoughtfully, "it's been called the Lost Dutchman's Mine for a really long time. A hundred and fifty years, right? So it can't be that easy to find."

"No," Henry agreed. "And I hid the saddlebag pretty well. I don't think they'll find that."

Simon and Henry climbed down from the fort to join Jack. They all crossed the yard to where Josie lay in the sun, tail twitching. Henry sat down next to her, stroking the warm fur between her ears. She purred agreeably and butted his hand when he stopped.

"I forgot to tell you!" he said to his brothers. "Josie was there last night. In the canyon. Delilah and I thought it was a wild animal, but it turned out to be Josie."

"She was? She goes up and down that mountain more often than we do!" Simon said admiringly. "So what's the deal with Delilah's dad?" he asked.

Henry hesitated. "He died in a car accident. When she was six."

"He DIED?" Jack looked horrified.

Henry nodded. "When she was about your age. That's why she's alone so much—her mom works, and there's nobody else. And that's why she got so upset about the compass—it belonged to her dad. And I looked for it everywhere when we were in the canyon, but I never could find it."

"We have to find it for her," Jack declared. "The next time."

Henry stared at him in disbelief, but before he could respond, Simon interjected, "You know what's interesting? Remember when we were at the graveyard? And Sara Delgado was saying all that weird stuff to us, stuff people say at funerals? That's why Delilah knew what she was talking about. Because of her dad."

Henry had forgotten that. He nodded slowly, running his fingers over Josie's long back.

"Did she get scared up on the mountain? Did she cry?" Simon asked.

"No," Henry answered honestly. "She didn't. Even though her leg hurt so much. Delilah is kind of *plucky*," he said thoughtfully.

"Yeah," Jack agreed. "She's pretty good, for a girl." He turned to Henry. "Did *you* get scared?"

"Yes," Henry said. "But then I got brave too." For the first time, he began to hope that maybe, just maybe, he had something more in common with Uncle Hank than simply a name.

"So when can we see Delilah again?" he asked Simon.

They drifted into a long debate about their mother's commitment to grounding them.

"Mom will get over it," Simon predicted. "We just worried her, you know?"

"Yeah," Henry agreed. "When she's worried, she always makes a lot of rules."

"So we'll stick close to home for a while," Simon said. "But that's okay. We can find out more about the Lost Dutchman's Mine. Then the next time we go up the mountain, we'll know what to look for."

"And we'll find the gold!" Jack added.

Simultaneously, they all three glanced at the mountain rising in the distance, a mystery of crags and woods and canyons, with its scattered bones and secret gold mines. Henry remembered the strangeness of the air, as urgent as someone breathing on the back of his neck. He flopped back on the grass, still stroking Josie's fur. The summer lay ahead of them, vast and uncharted . . . almost like a long, rocky passageway leading someplace new. Who could tell what secrets the mountain held? It would be up to them to find out.

AUTHOR'S NOTE

THERE ARE MANY unsolved mysteries of the American West, but the stories surrounding Superstition Mountain and the Lost Dutchman's Mine are especially intriguing. Could there be a better name than Superstition Mountain? It immediately suggests that this is a strange, spooky place. "The Superstitions," as the entire mountain range is called, are a rocky, high desert region of Arizona, full of cliffs, canyons, occasional groves of oak and pine trees, and the landmark Weaver's Needle. Their complicated past is peopled by Apache Indians and Spanish explorers, as well as soldiers, pioneers, and prospectors who came to the area looking to get rich.

While the town of Superstition and the contemporary characters in this novel are entirely fictional, all of the historical figures (such as Jacob Waltz and Adolph Ruth) are real, with the exception of Hank Cormody, the Barker boys' great-uncle. Artifacts like the Spanish coins are also based in fact. The record of disappearances and murders on the mountain is a subject of much debate, but the historical disappearances that are described here in detail—e.g.,

Adolph Ruth and his *"veni, vidi, vici"* note about the gold mine—are factual. The list that Henry finds in the back of the Superstition Mountain Historical Society pamphlet is compiled of recorded disappearances, some of them questionable, from various sources; the real-life list includes three teenagers from Texas who purportedly hiked up the mountain around 1950 and were never seen again.

To call Superstition Mountain a land equivalent of the Bermuda Triangle does not seem a stretch. It is a verifiably dangerous place, where even today visitors have to worry about getting lost and risking heatstroke, dehydration, and death. One of the most interesting things about the mountain is how often a few known details from the long-ago past (a Spaniard with a profitable gold mine) have given rise to elaborate legends (the famous Peralta Massacre). As historians have noted, all of the major components of the Superstition legends have at least some basis in fact.

As for the Lost Dutchman's Mine, it continues to attract gold seekers to the area. It too has been the subject of many stories and films, including the 1949 Glenn Ford movie *Lust for Gold* and a Scrooge McDuck tale by Don Rosa, "The Dutchman's Secret," in which Scrooge McDuck, Donald Duck, Huey, Dewey, and Louie go to Arizona in search of gold.

Does the mine really exist? Nobody knows. That is one more secret the mountain keeps.

ACKNOWLEDGMENTS

WITH LOVE AND HEARTFELT APPRECIATION, I would like to thank the following people for their help in the creation of this book:

My amazing editor, Christy Ottaviano, whom I am lucky to call a friend, and who has a rare talent for finding the bright jewel of a story in the morass of a rough draft, and then tenderly polishing it into being.

My wonderfully supportive agent, Edward Necarsulmer IV, an invaluable source of advice and a great advocate for my books.

The terrific team at Holt—from editorial to design to marketing to publicity to sales—whose enthusiasm, creativity, and hard work have carried my books to new heights.

My readers, some of whom are great writers themselves: Mary Broach, Jane Burns, Claire Carlson, Laura Forte, Jane Kamensky, Carol Sheriff, Zoe Wheeler, and my younger readers, Anna Daileader Sheriff, Justin Ferraro, and Jane Urheim. You guys are the best! You always ask the right questions, catch the continuity errors, and push the story where it needs to go. I am hugely in your debt. A special thanks to Carol's friend Laura Barry, associate curator of Prints, Maps, and Paintings at Colonial Williamsburg, for her help with the details of the map.

My beloved writing buddies, who patiently listened to many iterations of my *"Twin Peaks* for kids" idea, and whose funny insights about work, relationships, and life have permeated my stories at every turn, whether they realize it or not: Bennett Madison and Natalie Standiford, delightful companions through so many chatty New York lunches; Tony Abbott and Nora Raleigh Baskin, steadfast Blue Bird breakfast pals; Ellen Wittlinger, whose fondness for poetry, babies, and matchmaking mirrors my own; and Chris Tebbetts, my friend from the very beginning.

My friends who were generous enough to lend pretty homes in out-of-the-way spots for writing retreats that helped me finish the book: Elizabeth Bluemle, Sheila Clancy, and Jane Kamensky (once again!).

And finally, my family: my husband, Ward Wheeler, and children, Zoe, Harry, and Grace, who tolerate many inconveniences during the writing of a book, but who are ever-ready sources of honest feedback, inspiring plot twists, and lovely, much-needed distraction.

ABOUT THE AUTHOR

ELISE BROACH is the author of the award-winning books *Masterpiece* and *Shakespeare's Secret*; and *Desert Crossing*. She holds undergraduate and graduate degrees in history from Yale University. She lives with her family in Easton, Connecticut.

www.elisebroach.com

ABOUT THE ILLUSTRATOR

ANTONIO JAVIER CAPARO has illustrated many books for children, including The Magic Thief series and *The Young Reader's Shakespeare: A Midsummer Night's Dream*. He lives in Montreal, Canada.

www.antoniocaparo.com